Change hangs hea

As the *SS Calvin Coo* or,
Imogene gazed up at th ships looming on either side, and reality slapped her with a force that made her shudder.

Jimmy drew her close. But his embrace could not warm her chilled heart. All that Imogene had taken for granted—freedom, justice, love—seemed suddenly in jeopardy.

Gloom, dense as a coastal fog, fell on the entire ship the closer they came to Japan.

RACHEL DRUTEN is a native Californian. She is an artist as well as an author, wife, mother, and grandmother. Much of her time is devoted to overseeing a nonprofit, on-site, after-school program in the arts for disadvantaged children, K through 5.

Books by Rachel Druten

HEARTSONG PRESENTS
HP312—Out of the Darkness (with Dianna Crawford)
HP363—Rebellious Heart

Dark Side
of the Sun

Rachel Druten

Heartsong Presents

This book is dedicated to Dianna Crawford, mentor and friend, who gets me into trouble and out of it and is as good a Christian as you'll find anywhere.

A note from the author:
I love to hear from my readers! You may correspond with me by writing:

> **Rachel Druten**
> **Author Relations**
> **PO Box 719**
> **Uhrichsville, OH 44683**

ISBN 1-58660-622-0

DARK SIDE OF THE SUN

All Scripture quotations are taken from the King James Version of the Bible.

All of the characters and events in this book are fictitious. Any resemblance to actual persons, living or dead, or to actual events is purely coincidental.

Cover illustration by Jeff Whitlock.

PRINTED IN THE U.S.A.

one

October 30, 1941
San Pedro, California

"I hope this holds you until you get past the breakers." Daisy Fielding thrust a double box of See's chocolates into Imogene's hand and lipsticked her cheek with a good-bye kiss. She was Imogene's college roommate, best friend, and student teaching partner at Eagle Rock Elementary.

"Don't forget—" Daisy's last words were lost in the final blast of the ship's horn just above where they stood on the main deck of the *SS Calvin Coolidge*.

With mixed feelings, Imogene Pennington watched Daisy whirl and race down the ramp to join the little band of friends Imogene was about to leave behind. She looked forward to her trip home to the Philippines and her sister Becky's wedding, but three months was a long time, and she would miss her pals. Especially at Christmas.

The ship shuddered and began to move, her friends' good-byes blending with the cacophony of other shouting voices, the clank of the anchor being secured, the final strains of "God Bless America" being played by a small band on the wharf below. She leaned over the rail, watching as the large vessel slipped away from the dock and her friends grew smaller and smaller until they were out of sight. She watched the wharf buildings and cranes diminish in size and could only bring herself to turn away when the ship moved into the channel between the stone breakwaters.

She blinked back a recalcitrant tear. It was maddening the way her feelings were always so close to the surface. Given the right mood, even a cereal commercial on the radio could make her cry.

A crisp sea-scented breeze lifted the flared hem of her emerald green suit and tangled the tips of her sleek black pageboy. With one white-gloved hand, she reached up to adjust her matching beret. As she did, a pair of dervishes, eight or nine years old, in blue sailor suits barreled into her. Her cellophane-wrapped box of chocolates went flying—against the beam of the young Asian man standing next to her at the rail.

He straightened and turned.

Handsome! At least six feet tall with impressively broad shoulders under his blue blazer.

"I'm so sorry," Imogene exclaimed. "I hope it didn't hurt—"

Without so much as an acknowledgment, he bent to retrieve the box, thrust it back into her hand, and returned to his solitary rumination at the rail.

"Well, thank you." *So much for the good-neighbor policy.* She lifted her chin a proud notch and, clutching the box of sweets, strode toward the stairs.

৵

Jimmy Yamashida barely felt the bump and was hardly conscious of the young woman's apology, so deep was he into his own thoughts.

More than frustrated, he was furious that he had so suddenly and without explanation been called home to Japan. He would be missing the Stanford debate with Cal Berkeley and the rest of the football season. Coach had been less than pleased about that. He didn't blame him. And that wasn't the half of it.

Hunched over the ship's rail, he clenched and unclenched

his hands, remembering Dr. Gregson's explosion when he learned that Jimmy would not be singing the baritone solo in Handel's *Messiah*.

"And who do you think will replace you?" the angry conductor had stormed.

The weight of the man's wrath still hung heavy.

But the choice had not been Jimmy's.

He had tried to reason with his father to let him stay. At least through Christmas. To no avail.

"Come home at once, Jimmu. We will not discuss it!" His father's strength of will rang clear, despite the static on the line of the trans-Pacific phone call. As usual, his father, the powerful businessman, expected the same total obedience from Jimmy he demanded from everyone else.

The long-distance operator had cut in. The line disconnected.

A young Japanese man did not argue with his elders.

But Jimmy had spent most of the last twelve of his twenty-two years in the United States—first in boarding school and now as a graduate student at Stanford University. As a result, he had begun to feel less like a Japanese and more like an American. It was getting harder and harder to accept the traditions and customs of his homeland. To say nothing of its politics. Japan's invasion of China was a subject he dared not broach with his father.

As the sun, bright orange, slipped beneath the horizon, Jimmy turned from his absent perusal of the sea and walked toward the stairs.

No, his father would not be pleased with the result of his son's American education.

One of the largest shipbuilders in Japan, his father had sent Jimmy to the United States to learn the American mind. "You are to return prepared to help your homeland assume its rightful place as a world industrial power."

The lessons had taken all too well.

⋟

Talk about a fellow who was self-absorbed. The Occidental College homecoming princess was not used to being treated with such indifference. Still smarting from the young man's slight, Imogene, skirt swinging, strode along the corridor toward her stateroom.

As she thrust the door open, her gaze fell on a tremendous bouquet of red roses on the desk beneath the porthole. Tossing her beret beside her purse on the bed, she laid the box of chocolates next to the flowers, then removed her gloves, finger by finger, as she leaned forward to study the attached card.

It was from Ted.

She certainly couldn't complain about *Ted's* attention. Though he'd been unable to see her off at the boat, he'd sent this lavish bouquet. "As a lingering good-bye," the note began. It continued with his declaration of devotion and promise to be faithful.

Imogene smiled at that one. She knew his pledge wouldn't last until the Christmas formal. No, Ted was not one to miss the biggest party season of the year.

He was a great dancer. She snapped his note between her fingers. "I wonder if the swing is as popular in Manila as it is in California."

She turned. Other, more important thoughts intervened— like which dress to wear to the captain's party that evening.

⋟

Imogene glided into the spacious, wood-paneled lounge filled with elegantly-attired passengers and a sumptuous profusion of potted plants and bright flowers on the scattering of small linen-covered tables. Artfully arranged around the perimeter of the room were groupings of red plush overstuffed chairs and love seats, and at the grand piano in the corner a tuxedo-clad young man was playing a medley of show tunes as background music.

As she strolled toward the buffet table, she felt quite glamorous in her cranberry brocade mandarin sheath with its side-slit skirt. Dark hair grazed her shoulders, and a subtle touch of mascara accentuated the upward slant of her exotic violet eyes.

She was alone, young, and—if reports could be believed—not all that disagreeable looking, despite what that rude young man might have thought. Her gaze scanned the room. Unfortunately he wasn't there to see her entrance.

Stewards in their white jackets, black trousers, and bow ties wove among the guests passing out hot hors d'oeuvres and offering glasses of champagne.

"May I get you something, Miss?"

"Just ice water, please."

"Nothin' stronger?" a brash male voice bellowed.

If all eyes hadn't been on her before, they certainly were now.

"It's a party, little miss. Just water ain't much fun." The flush-faced man, his tux jacket straining across his belly, moved closer. The cocktail he held sloshed over the side of the glass as he switched it from one hand to the other and extended a beefy paw toward Imogene. "Raymond Diller," he boomed. "In kapok—you know, the stuff you fill mattresses with. Export it out of the Philippines. This here is the little woman, Denice. Who did you say you were?" He cocked his ear toward Imogene.

Hesitantly she took his damp hand and murmured her name.

"Say hello to Imogene Pennington," Raymond commanded his wife, loud enough for nearby heads to turn.

The pale but pretty little blond woman, with an opal brooch

the size of the moon on her pink lace sheath, returned a wan smile. Her eyes reflected helpless acceptance.

"Call me Ray," he invited, trying for a charming smile and achieving a leer. "I'm headin' back to the islands to clear up some business, and then we'll hightail it home to Texas before war breaks out with the Japs."

Imogene frowned. She'd never been much interested in politics. Of course she knew the Japanese had invaded China a few years before and, in the abstract, disapproved. But it hardly affected her. "If my father had thought war imminent between the United States and Japan, I doubt he would have allowed me to come home."

"Then he's a fool." The man gestured with his cocktail. "Mark my word—"

"Please, Dahlin'—not everyone shares your opinion." His wife placed her hand timidly on his arm.

"Now look what you made me do," he growled, glaring at the puddle of liquid staining the red carpet.

"I'm sorry, Dahlin'. I thought I barely touched you."

Imogene noticed that his was not the only drink to spill. Ever since she'd entered the lounge, she had sensed a persistently growing motion, which was probably not as evident to most of the other guests who, by then, were well into the celebration of their voyage. But suddenly the ship had taken on a more emphatic movement, a heave and shudder that caused her to grasp the edge of the chair beside her.

Platters of canapés and fruit slid from the buffet table. An ice-sculptured Venus teetered dangerously in her sea of caviar and fell into the arms of an alert steward.

There was an instant of silence, then nervous laughter, and the room broke out in a babble of excited voices as stewards scurried about, tackling the mess with professional aplomb.

The captain disengaged himself from a group in the corner and stepped forward, his voice replete with soothing calm and studied reassurance. "It appears we have hit a bit of a storm. We should ride it out quite nicely." With a deprecating smile, he added, "Unpleasant as it may seem at the moment, it will soon be merely an entertaining source of conversation."

With that the ship heaved and fell again, causing even the stalwart captain to stumble and the passengers who were left standing to slide and scatter.

Undaunted, a half-hour later, Imogene stood gazing into the grand teak-paneled dining room. It sparkled in the refracted light of beveled mirrors, swinging chandeliers, and cut-crystal vases and goblets.

She counted ten linen-draped tables for eight, formally set, each napkin folded into a swan. And not one seat occupied. On a tiny stage in the center of the room stood a harp. But no musician. Only she and one stalwart, white-jacketed steward occupied the elegant room.

In the three times Imogene had made the Pacific crossing, she'd not encountered a storm as powerful as this one. The ship rose and fell like the roller coaster at the Long Beach Pike. But, as always, her stomach was up to the challenge. Alone at her table, she polished off a six-course dinner that included foie gras, beef Wellington, and a luscious éclair for dessert.

"Excellent service." She smiled at the steward as she prepared to leave, only to be tossed back down into her chair. Finally, with his help and the aid of a pillar, a table, and a nearby chair, she managed to lurch out of the dining room.

The wind howled around her as she maneuvered the covered deck, keeping a sturdy grip on the rail. She could almost feel the chill spray that smashed against the glass screening her from the storm.

All dressed up and nowhere to go, she thought peevishly, as she wandered back into the lounge. By now, everything movable had been battened down and the breakables tucked safely away. The lounge, like the dining room, was deserted and almost silent, insulated from the wail of the storm.

Almost silent, but not quite.

The mellifluous tones of a baritone voice drifted over the back of a high, wingback chair, half-humming, half-singing music with which Imogene was more than familiar. She had often accompanied the Occidental Glee Club in a medley of Brahms folk songs in which that very song had been included.

The moment was irresistible.

She moved to the piano and sat down, allowing her fingers to drift over the keys.

When the final notes had died, there was a lingering pause. She felt a bubble of excitement. And suspense. She leaned forward in anticipation, peeking toward the wingback chair as the dark figure arose.

A surge of disappointment swept through her. "Oh, it's you."

The young man frowned, peered down at his polished shoes, his black knife-pleated trousers. He examined his black satin cummerbund, his tux jacket, and gold-studded cuffs. "Yes, you're absolutely right. I do believe it is me," he said with certainty, then cocked a grin. "How astute of you."

two

Astute? How arrogant.

"Hello," he said.

Imogene's nose lifted a notch. "We've already met."

He looked puzzled.

"You saved my box of chocolates. I tried to thank you, but you were—" She shrugged.

"Otherwise occupied?"

"Clearly."

He gave her a sheepish smile. "I'm sorry."

She had noticed his height and his broad shoulders and that he was more than passingly handsome. What she had missed was the impact of his dark, expressive eyes.

One deep breath and she decided to forgive him.

"How did you know those Brahms folk songs?" he asked, moving toward her. "They're not often played on the jukebox."

"I accompany my college glee club. It's a medley we sing. Where did you learn them?"

"In *my* college glee club." By now he had reached the piano. "I really must have been *very* preoccupied," he said, his expression admiring, "not to have noticed you."

"You didn't seem very happy."

The smile slid from his eyes. "You're right. Home for the holidays, and I was thinking of all I'll be missing."

"Me, too. Where's home?"

"Japan. You?"

13

"The Philippines. Negros Island. My father owns a copra plantation in Pamplona."

"Mine builds—boats. So what college glee club do you accompany?" he asked, abruptly changing the subject.

"Occidental College."

Builds boats? Big? Small? Big! He could afford to give his son an American education and bring him home first-class.

"Where do you go to school?"

"I'm a grad student at Stanford." He leaned against the piano and crossed his arms. "I know Occidental. You have a great track team."

"Do you run track?"

"Football. We had a chance for the championship this year."

"Had?"

"Well, *have*, I suppose," he said dolefully.

"Even without you?" she teased.

He shrugged.

He certainly had the build for a football player. She swallowed. Not all Japanese athletes had to be sumo wrestlers.

"Let me guess." She leaned her elbow on her crossed knee. Resting her chin in her hand, she assessed him. "You're certainly not a tackle—and not big enough for a back." She straightened. "I'd say you're either a quarterback or an end."

His grin told her she had hit the mark.

"Which is it?"

"End. You know your football. I'm impressed."

Suddenly shy in the beam of his admiring gaze, Imogene murmured, "One doesn't have to play a game to understand it."

"No," he replied, and their gazes held.

"So you're their star end who catches all the passes," she said lightly, breaking the spell.

He assumed a modest expression. "I caught my share, I hope."

"Enough so they'll miss you?"

He shrugged again, but his grin told her they would.

"I'm Imogene Pennington." She extended her hand.

Taking it in his, the young man bowed slightly. "Jimmu Yamashida—Jimmy." And he continued to hold her hand, as his dark eyes smiled into hers.

His grasp was firm but gentle, and she thought his eyes gentle, too, and honest. He had the eyes of a man one could trust.

The momentary calm suddenly erupted into a heave that sent Imogene rocking across the piano bench. Only Jimmy's tightened grip kept her from sliding off completely.

"Perhaps we can find you a safer place to sit," he said, taking her arm. "Or we could go to the ballroom. I daresay there'll be plenty of room on the dance floor."

"It's still open?"

"And there's a combo. I looked in after dinner."

"You weren't in the dining room, unless you were at the first seating."

"No, the second one, but the dining room was empty when I looked, so I had my dinner sent to my cabin. It's not much fun to eat alone."

"A minute later and you wouldn't have been alone." She cast him a sweet smile.

He was about to reply when another dip sent her staggering against him. His arm swept around her.

She giggled nervously. "Already we're dancing, and we've yet to hear the music."

They lurched down the long, carpeted corridor, arm in arm, until they finally reached the ballroom.

It was suitably dim, with a stage and dance floor and a faceted glass ball spinning out minuscule rainbows of fractured light.

On stage the trio—drums, a piano, and a bass—swayed more from the motion of the sea than the music, but neither the couple holding hands at a nearby table nor the lone man sitting next to the dance floor seemed to notice or care. Nor did Imogene or Jimmy, who found their own private corner.

"That was quick," Jimmy remarked, as the steward returned with their beverages almost immediately. "But then it wasn't a complicated order." He lifted his drink. "Cheers."

As their glasses met, so did their gazes.

Imogene took a sip. "You don't have an accent. Were you born in America?"

"No. In Japan. But from the time I can remember, I was tutored in English. Then I was sent to boarding school in the States. And, of course, Stanford."

"So you've spent more time in America than in Japan."

"Since I was ten." He took a sip of his cola.

"But still Japanese is such a different language from English that I'd expect some residual inflection or cadence."

Jimmy smiled. "That's the musician in you speaking. I'm glad to know I achieved my goal so successfully."

"To lose your accent?"

"To lose the slightest vestiges of it. As a kid I wanted to fit in. I couldn't do anything about my looks, but I could about my accent."

Silently Imogene studied him, seeing the lonely child he must have been, far away from family and friends, thrust into an atmosphere so completely foreign. A bit as she felt when she'd first come stateside. Until her loving friends at Occidental College had taken her under their wings.

"So you became a cultural chameleon," she said.

"I never thought of it like that. But, yes, I suppose I did."

"And now you're going home to Japan, where you will

become Japanese again." Her voice was quiet.

"Unless I jump ship in Hawaii."

⋅❧⋅

He didn't want to go back. That was the truth of it. Deep down inside, Jimmy had an ominous feeling that he would never return to America.

As he gazed into Imogene's large, violet eyes, eyes so filled with warmth and understanding, he realized how much would be lost to him. Suddenly the young woman sitting before him became a symbol of that loss. He wanted to hold onto her for what she represented, individuality, joy—freedom.

He wanted to hold onto her for what she was, beautiful and compassionate.

At Stanford he was a minority of one and as such, acceptable. He spent weekends with friends in Hillsborough but knew enough not to ask out their sisters. He dated Mills College girls but was rarely taken home to meet their families.

But here was this beautiful young woman, intriguing, with a mysterious hint of the Eurasian about her, cosmopolitan, intelligent, who seemed to see him not as a Japanese, but as a man.

He stood and reached for her hand. "Let's dance."

❧

Imogene melted so easily, so naturally into Jimmy's arms. The combo was playing "Bye Bye Blues," and the two moved together, feeling as one the languid rhythm of the slow, syncopated beat, holding each other as the ship dipped and rose, not wanting to let go. Laughing when a sudden jolt sent them spinning, clinging.

"This is getting dangerous," she giggled.

He leaned back, smiling into her eyes. "So I'm learning more about Miss Imogene. Willing to face danger. She's not only beautiful but brave."

"Or reckless."

The man who had been sitting alone at the table arose and moved toward them on unsteady legs. "Jimmu, old man." His speech was thick, his accent British.

"Didn't recognize you from the back, Langston—though I should have."

He was taller than Jimmy and heavier. A shock of white-blond hair fell across his thick brow, and his blue eyes were so pale as to be almost transparent. "Only fair you should share the wealth." He gave Imogene a crooked smile and grabbed her arm. His teeth were as bad as his breath.

"I think not." Jimmy pivoted away, placing himself between the man and her.

The man stumbled forward. "Daddy wouldn't like that."

"Daddy isn't here," Jimmy growled. "Now get lost."

"Jus' doin' my job," the man persisted, lurching after them.

"Your job does not include annoying the lady." Jimmy pulled Imogene from the dance floor and toward their table.

She felt his anger in the grip of his hand and the fierceness of his stride. She saw it in his narrowed eyes.

Once she was seated, he turned on his aggressor. And, although he pulled the man away and his voice was low, she could hear his words, measured, precise. "You can do your job in the United States; you can do it in Japan. But on this ship you'll leave me alone, or you'll find yourself floating in the Pacific." He swung the man around and, with the help of the storm, sent him stumbling through the door.

Jimmy's face was still grim as he sat down across from her.

"You—you didn't really mean that, did you? The part about throwing him in the Pacific?" Imogene asked, overwhelmed with the possibility that he might. After all, what did she know about Jimmu Yamashida except what he himself had told her?

Jimmy laughed, a short, harsh laugh, but his expression relaxed. "Of course I didn't mean it." He covered her fingers reassuringly with his. "Would you have asked that question if you thought I did?"

Imogene paused. "Well, it did cross my mind. But, I guess, no."

He squeezed her hand and smiled, the warm, diffident smile she found so beguiling.

She knew she should let the incident drop. Clearly Jimmy was ready to. But curiosity got the better of her. "Who is he?"

"A friend of my father's" was the short, unsatisfactory reply, as Jimmy withdrew his hand and lifted his glass.

It was well after midnight, although Imogene could hardly believe it. They walked along the promenade, her arm linked in his as he held onto the rail, the wind howling around them. Through the steaming glass an occasional flash of lightning defined the slanting horizon and the frothing sea.

The ship creaked and strained and suddenly fell.

Jimmy swung Imogene around, imprisoning her with his arms, as his hands clutched tightly to the rail on either side. He was pitched against her, then thrust away from the too-familiar closeness.

Arms entwined around the other's waist, they finally wove their way back along the enclosed deck, giggling, bumping against the walls, holding each other up against the bucking storm.

"Like a couple of drunken sailors, if I didn't know better," Jimmy said.

Imogene could have partied all night. The pressure of propriety was the only reason she'd insisted on ending the evening. "I think you brought me the long way home," she observed, smiling up into his eyes.

"Why wouldn't I? I don't want this night to end. In fact," he said softly, leaning against her stateroom door and gazing down at her, "I'd not complain if it went on forever."

The warmth in his gaze and the low timbre of his voice set off an alarming and unfamiliar response in Imogene.

Her heart fluttered.

Always it had been she who was in control. She knew very well a young man's fancy and how to captivate him. Now it was as if her own wiles were being used against her.

She lowered her eyes. She didn't know where to look.

His high-polished shoes? His satin cummerbund? The front of his starched white shirt?

Her breath caught.

His jaw. His lips. She couldn't seem to drag her gaze any higher than his lips. Sculpted, firm, mobile.

three

Imogene squinched down under the covers, savoring those languorous, delicious moments between sleep and wakefulness.

She wrapped her arms around herself, remembering the night before, the feel of Jimmy's embrace as they danced, his cheek against hers, the sound of his voice, his lips—yet to touch hers.

Probably for the best. As American as he seemed, they came from very different worlds.

She took a deep breath that ended in a sigh.

Stretching, she rolled over and snapped up the blind. Through the porthole, a beam of light cast an oval of gold on her blanket and bathed the room in morning sunshine.

They had ridden out the storm.

After a leisurely shower, she dressed in a blue-and-white shirtmaker blouse and white pleated skirt and slipped into a pair of sandals. Then, tying her hair back in a matching blue ribbon, she added a touch of rouge to her cheeks and a taste of color to her lips and was ready to meet the day.

What a luxury it was not to rush. At school she had always arrived breathless for her eight o'clock class.

She glanced at her watch. Too late to be served breakfast, she headed for the buffet on the top deck provided for lazy risers like herself. Still, as she passed the dining room, she peeked in to see if Jimmy might be there.

He wasn't.

She felt the gentle swells of a calm sea as she strolled toward the stairs. Sunlight glittered across the water like millions of newly minted dimes tossed across its surface. She paused, allowing the fresh, cool spray to dampen her cheeks and the sun to dry them.

Nor was Jimmy at the buffet.

At first the disappointment did not affect her appetite. She quaffed her orange juice with gusto. But as she attacked her Denver omelet and still saw no sign of him, she began to have second thoughts.

Maybe she had just been last night's diversion for him. What other choices had he? Everybody else was seasick. Anyway, he probably preferred Japanese girls.

Just as well.

She took a sip of coffee.

Maybe he'd found one.

By then she had talked herself into the blues so deep that she couldn't even finish her second piece of toast.

After three brisk circles around the entire deck and still no Jimmy, her doubts became serious.

Weary more from disillusionment than physical exertion, she fell into her assigned deck chair and closed her eyes.

"Bouillon, Miss?"

Without looking up, she waved the steward off. "No, thank you."

"You're sure?"

"I just had breakfast." She put her forearm over her eyes, hoping he'd get the message.

"It's very nutritious," he persisted.

Couldn't he see she wanted to be left alone? But—that voice. Her eyes snapped open.

Jimmy gave her a beleaguered smile. "When you weren't at breakfast, I figured I'd come on too fast last night. Frightened you away." He stood above her, a white tennis sweater thrown over the shoulders of his green polo shirt. He held a tray containing two cups of bouillon and a nosegay—of all things. "I just want to assure you that you can count on me to be a perfect gentleman."

Jimmy eased down onto the empty lounge beside her. "These are for you." He handed her the flowers.

"Forget-me-nots. How lovely."

"Small but sentimental."

"Perfect."

"I try."

"Which makes me fear you've had a great deal of practice." She observed him through a sweep of dark lashes.

"Not so."

"I can hardly believe that. You have such an easy patter, and you're such a good dancer. And you know exactly what will please a lady—"

"Would you belittle the gift by doubting my sincerity?" he asked lightly.

"I'm sorry. You're right." She could see that despite his easy manner, his eyes reflected a touch of wounded pride. She looked down at the nosegay. "You have no idea how much trouble I cause with my teasing," she murmured. "It's absolutely one of my worst faults."

Jimmy laughed. "Well, if that's as bad as it gets, you don't have much to worry about." He handed her a cup of bouillon, took the other for himself, and slid the tray beneath his deck chair.

"Cheers," he toasted, lifting his cup.

"You'd better not get too comfortable," Imogene warned. "These deck chairs are assigned, you know."

"I know." He gave her a self-satisfied smirk and settled back.

"Well, mercy me," Imogene trilled, "and yours is next to mine. What an *amazing* coincidence."

And so the day went. They jaunted around the deck in chaste communion, without the excuse of a storm allowing them to touch. She challenged him to a game of deck tennis. He challenged her to shuffleboard. Instead of lunch in the dining room, they ordered from the steward, eating on trays, side by side on their assigned deck chairs. When they were offered a game of bridge, he declined. He whispered to her that he wasn't ready yet to share her. So they played backgammon in the lounge until passengers began gathering for afternoon tea—at which time they fled.

Jimmy, his elbows resting on the rail, his hands clasped in front of him, gazed thoughtfully at the sea.

Imogene gazed at Jimmy.

His fine-shaped head and classic profile made her think of the romantic heroes she had fantasized about. His ears were neat against his thick black hair, his features straight and chiseled. Above his passionate midnight eyes, raven brows slashed against his golden skin, bronzed darker by the late afternoon sun.

She sighed. He reminded her of the picture of a samurai warrior she'd seen in a storybook as a child.

But the eyes he turned on her were not hard or cruel. He reached over and brushed back a lock of hair that had blown across her cheek.

Her gentle samurai.

"You never told me why your father wanted you to leave school in the middle of the term," she said.

"He didn't say."

"You mean he just ordered you to come home with no reason at all?"

"My father is never without a reason."

"But he wouldn't explain why?" She could hardly believe, in this day and age, that a father could get away with that. Certainly hers couldn't, not with two mouthy daughters who never gave up.

"In Japan a father need not explain." Jimmy grimaced slightly. "In Japan a son obeys his father without question."

"My dad would love that." Imogene shook her head and smiled. She glanced at the sun and then at her watch. "Oh, my, I need to change for dinner."

They turned and began walking the promenade toward the stairs. "So, with all the unrest, why are you going back to the Philippines?" Jimmy asked.

Imogene remembered a similar observation from Mr. Diller, though not so nicely put.

"My sister's wedding. Daddy wasn't anxious to have me make the trip, but I convinced him." She smiled. "You know how daddies are with their little girls. Besides, it's been two years since I've seen them. I miss them."

"What about your classes?"

"I am taking the semester off." She shrugged. "What about you?"

Jimmy looked away, his face pensive. "It would seem I am, too." He turned back to her. "I don't want to talk about it. Do you mind? Let's—let's talk only about now."

They had reached her stateroom, and the gaze that met hers was troubled. He took her hand. "Last night was fantastic. But today has been. . .it was. . .well, I've never had a day like it." Absently, as he spoke, his thumb traced her hand.

Taking a deep, calming breath, she closed her fingers around his. "And there's still the evening to look forward to," she said softly.

જ

Her gleaming hair swept back into a chignon, Imogene wafted into the dining room in a faint cloud of perfume, wearing a violet tunic the color of her eyes. It shimmered over a long, black satin skirt. Her ears were studded with simple earrings that matched the rope of pearls around her neck.

Judging from the admiring glances cast in her direction, she had scored again.

As she moved toward her assigned table, a steward intercepted her. "The seating arrangement has been changed, Miss. If you'll follow me, please."

The gentlemen at her new table rose as she was escorted to the place next to, whom else, Jimmy.

"Another amazing coincidence," she murmured as Jimmy pushed in her chair. "How did you manage?"

"It was easy." He tilted his head toward her originally assigned table. In her spot sat the large obnoxious blond man who'd caused the ruckus in the ballroom. "He was happy to do me a favor."

"What makes me think he's something besides a friend of your father?" Imogene drew her napkin onto her lap. "One of these days—"

"We have much more interesting things to talk about than him," Jimmy whispered.

It was the first night without a storm since the voyage began, and their table was complete. These were the folks she would be dining with the rest of the trip, and to her dismay they included Raymond and Denice Diller.

Well, she guessed it didn't matter as long as Jimmy was beside her.

Agatha Duke, a large-boned, stylishly aristocratic-looking dowager with an important nose, sat to Imogene's right. When they had exchanged introductions, she asked, "Is your father Will Pennington?"

Imogene nodded.

"He is highly respected throughout the islands, you know."

From the tone of the words, Imogene sensed being related to Will Pennington brought her up a notch in Mrs. Duke's esteem.

"He and my husband, Babcock, have worked on engineering projects together—we're connected to the Angier Babcock Dukes," she confided. "That's why we honored our son with the name Angier. Have you met my dear son?"

A pale, listless version of Mrs. Duke sat opposite Imogene at the round table.

"I don't believe so," she murmured, recognizing a predatory gleam in his mother's eyes.

"Angie." The gull-like squawk of the woman's voice cut through the other conversations, and all eyes turned. "You and Miss Pennington have something in common. Both your fathers are engineers. Perhaps after dinner you can get acquainted."

And discuss our fathers? Imogene exchanged glances with Jimmy.

Angier's eye twitched in her direction.

Poor fellow. A domineering mother like Mrs. Duke would cause anyone to twitch.

"I'd like that—to get better acquainted."

His nasal, obsequious tone was even more disagreeable than his mother's squawk, and yet Imogene's heart went out to the shy, unattractive young man.

As the first course was being served, a Miss Goldie Yoder, seated next to Mrs. Duke, kindly introduced the others at the table.

Mrs. Duke lifted her fork. "Ah, Fonds d'Artichauts au Caviar.

One of my favorites." But after a bite she wrinkled her nose. "Much more subtle at Romanoff's, however."

Imogene, who existed largely on college cuisine and Bob's Big Boy burgers, was not about to quibble over artichoke hearts with caviar.

"Caviar again!" Raymond Diller complained loud enough to be heard in the kitchen. "It gets me how people can be so impressed. They're just fish eggs, after all."

"Shh," his wife whispered. Her delicate, pale hand fluttered toward his arm.

"Don't shush me, Denice!" he boomed. "I call it as I see it. And I think caviar should be fed to the cats. That's my opinion, and I'm sticking to it."

"He must be a bit hard of hearing," Jimmy whispered.

"You're being charitable," Imogene whispered back. "Now I know why you wanted me here. To share the misery."

He squeezed her hand under the table. "That's not the only reason, but it'll do for now."

As the steward removed her polished plate, Imogene noticed Mrs. Duke had cleaned hers, too. Despite the woman's lamentation, not a single spot of caviar was left on her plate either.

"My dear," she said, leaning close to Imogene and whispering under her breath, "since I have such admiration for your father and can see what a lovely young lady you are, may I give you a word of advice?" Without waiting for a reply, she continued. "I've observed that young Mr. Yamashida seems to be taking an inordinate interest in you. Do you think your father would approve? Mr. Yamashida being Oriental and all."

Imogene nearly choked on the water she was swallowing. The audacity! And from a perfect stranger.

She glanced at Jimmy to see if he had overheard, but fortunately it seemed not, as he was engaged in conversation with

Mrs. Nickleson, an elderly lady to his right.

She turned back to Mrs. Duke. In a tone so saccharine sweet it cloyed, she replied, "I know my father would appreciate your concern, Mrs. Duke, but as my mother was half Filipino, I doubt he'd object too strenuously. And as he so often says, it's not accident of birth but character that counts. Don't you agree?"

"Hear, hear," murmured Miss Yoder, on the other side of Mrs. Duke.

"Of course—naturally," Mrs. Duke mumbled. "Character is of prime importance." She patted her lips with the corner of her napkin. "Ah, Potage Crecy a la Tomate," she observed, abruptly turning her attention to the soup course being served. "I hope it's better than the Fonds d'Artichauts au Caviar."

"This is more like it," Mr. Diller announced. "Good old-fashioned tomato soup."

"I think it's tomato and carrot, Dahlin'," Mrs. Diller warned nervously.

"Wouldn't you know it." He slapped his spoon back into the bowl, splashing spots of pink on the white linen cloth. "They have to go and mess up perfectly good tomato soup with carrots. I can't stand carrots."

Miss Yoder, sitting between him and Mrs. Duke, gave him a sweet smile. "It's delicious, Mr. Diller," she said gently. "You should try it."

Miss Goldie Yoder, with her dimpled, unlined face and curly gray-blond hair, smiled with the sweetness of a middle-aged Shirley Temple.

Raymond Diller took a grudging sip. "Not bad," he admitted. Between swallows he continued to eye Jimmy with a stalking gleam, as he had since the dinner began.

The other predator at the table, Imogene thought, although she knew Mrs. Duke had an entirely different agenda.

Then he pounced. "So what do you American Japs think about the world situation?" He ladled another spoonful of soup into his mouth and wiped a drip from his chin. "Although I suppose a Jap is a Jap wherever he's born."

Imogene's shoulders stiffened. She couldn't look at Jimmy.

"Denice." The man turned sharply to his wife. "Will you stop kicking me. He knows it's not personal."

"As a matter of fact, I was born in Japan. I'm a Japanese citizen," Jimmy said mildly.

"Could have fooled me." The man grunted as he put down his spoon. "But then that's the point, isn't it?"

Mrs. Nickleson, who had been dozing between the soup course and the entrée, leaned over to Denice Diller. "What did he say?"

"Nothin' important," Mrs. Diller replied, sending her husband an imploring glance.

"Don't give me that look, Denice. I call it as I see it." He turned his coarse, flushed face back to Jimmy. "So how do you justify your rape of Nanking and the invasion of Indochina?" As if Jimmy were to blame.

Angier Duke cleared his throat and looked down at his plate.

Even his mother seemed embarrassed as she toyed with her napkin.

Denice Diller looked as if she were about to cry.

And Mrs. Nickleson had dozed off again, missing the whole thing.

Miss Yoder's clear, soft voice suddenly cut through the silence. "I don't believe we can hold Mr. Yamashida responsible for the actions of his government, Mr. Diller. I am well aware of the brutality of which you speak. But as a Presbyterian missionary in Japan for most of my life, I have experienced quite another side, a courteous, thoughtful, reverent side of the Japanese character."

But the bully was not about to retreat. "What you're saying is that not every Jap is a bloodthirsty, warmongering brute. I'll buy that. Not *all* of them." He smirked.

That did it! Imogene jumped to her feet, her chair crashing to the floor behind her. Her voice rang out in righteous indignation. "Just as all Americans are not insensitive boors, *Mr. Diller.*"

The whole dining room shivered into silence. All eyes focused on Imogene.

Furious, yet horrified by her spontaneous outburst, she thrust aside Jimmy's restraining hand and ran out of the dining room, down the deck. She crashed past strolling passengers, stumbled over deck chairs, her loosened hair flying like a thick, black banner behind her.

Finally finding sanctuary behind the lifeboats, she burst into tears.

And then she felt his arms around her, the touch of his hands, smoothing her hair, and his soothing voice, whispering against her cheek.

"Don't cry, sweet girl. What does it matter what he thinks?"

"It's not just him. It's Mrs. Duke, too. All of them. They're so prejudiced, so cruel. Oh, J–Jimmy. In the Philippines it's not like that at all." Her words came out in little sobbing sighs. "It's so unfair. They don't even know you."

"I know—I know," he soothed, rocking her in his arms.

Imogene sank into his embrace. She curled into his arms, her head against his chest, comforted by his heart's beat and his gentle, stroking hand against her hair. "I feel safe when I'm with you. And I feel as if I can be myself. I'm sure they're all in there right now saying something just as bad about me.

When I told Mrs. Duke that my mother was part Filipino, you should have seen the way she looked at me."

"Are you going to let what that woman thinks bother you? Why, you're the most beautiful, perfect girl I've ever known."

But Jimmy's reassuring, tender words barely registered. Imogene was too overwrought. "They're all such hypocrites— all of them," she sobbed, wetting the front of his pleated shirt with her tears. "I hate them."

He lifted her face and smoothed back the damp strands of hair clinging to her cheek. In the dim light she could see his brow furrowed, his face sad and troubled. "Don't judge them too harshly, Imogene. Believe me, the Americans don't have a monopoly on prejudice. And as for what's going on in Japan, even I have difficulty reconciling what I'm hearing about my government." He gazed out toward the sea, as if somehow he would find the answers there.

Then he looked down at her and said lightly, "Miss Yoder certainly isn't a hypocrite. And Angier looked pretty upset at what Mr. Diller was saying—"

"But his mother didn't," Imogene said fiercely.

"We can't judge him by his mother. And certainly we shouldn't blame poor Mrs. Diller for her husband's behavior—"

"Who knows what she thinks? She never gets a word in edgewise."

"And I'm sure Mrs. Nickleson doesn't agree—"

"How would you know? She slept through the whole conversation. Oh, Jimmy!" Imogene wailed. "You're so forgiving. So good." She wanted to protect him from people like Raymond Diller—and Mrs. Duke.

Suddenly she realized that for her, at least, this wasn't just another shipboard romance.

She really cared about him.

Vaguely she was aware of the muffled hum of the engines far below and the soft slap of waves hitting the hull. In the fragrant, cool breeze she felt his warmth.

And, for that instant, she felt as if nothing could touch them.

But the feeling didn't last. "Oh, Jimmy," she sobbed, "everything is so confusing." She leaned back in his arms and gazed into his dear face, cast in silver by the moon.

Her gentle samurai.

He lowered his head and kissed her, a kiss so tender she thought her heart would burst.

Imogene threw her arms around him, clung to him, returning his embrace with such fierce longing. As if this first kiss were to be their last.

❧

Mr. Diller was a mean, insensitive bully. How could he treat Jimmy so abominably? He'd tried to humiliate him publicly. Imogene knew she would never forgive him. Much as she prayed, she could not quell the anger, the hate—yes, the hate—she harbored in her heart against him.

She slept with it that night and woke with it in the morning.

She knew what the Bible said. "Love your enemies and pray for those who persecute you—"

But she couldn't.

Then, when she picked up her Bible that Sunday morning, she suddenly felt as much a hypocrite as she had accused others of being.

And much worse. She realized she was falling in love with a man who didn't share her faith.

Jimmy was the only one at their table when Imogene arrived for breakfast, and despite her troubling insight, she was thrilled to see him. As he seated her, his hand touched hers for just an instant, and the look in his eyes told her the depth of his feelings more than any words could.

The steward poured coffee and handed them each a menu, which Imogene put down without opening.

"You're not ordering?"

She shook her head. "I'm not hungry." Not for food. She just wanted to be near him.

"That's not like you."

She returned his smile. He was right. It had been only a few days, and already he knew what she was like.

"What are you reading?" he asked, glancing at the book in her lap.

"My Bible. It's Sunday. I'm going to the morning service."

"So it is. I'd forgotten. I'm afraid in college I got out of the church habit," he said sheepishly.

Imogene put down her cup. Had she heard correctly? "You're a *Christian?*"

"Well, sort of. I guess."

He might know a lot about her, but it seemed she still had much to learn about him. "You can't be sort of. You either are or you're not."

He grinned. "I guess you could say I'm a Christian in my mother's house. At college I'm a sort of." He leaned his elbow on the table and rested his cheek in his hand, gazing deeply into her eyes.

Garnering a modicum of composure, she said, "I thought the Japanese were Shintos."

"Shinto is the state religion. It's taught in school." He took a swallow of coffee. "But people can also be Buddhists or Confucianists, Taoists. Even Christians. As a matter of fact, Christianity has been in Japan since the middle of the sixteenth century."

"Well, aren't you the walking encyclopedia."

"And a Christian."

"Of sorts."

It seemed so was she. She'd been reminded just this morning. The steward refilled their coffee cups.

As Jimmy lifted his, he asked, "May I go with you?"

"To church?" Her heart was so full. Suddenly there didn't seem any room left for anger and hate. Even against Mr. Diller. "Oh, Jimmy, of course you can."

As the steward arrived to take their order, Miss Yoder hurried into the dining room, her gray-blond curls bobbing. Her sweet face, so serene the night before, was filled with anguish. "Oh, my dears, have you heard the news?"

"What news?" they asked in unison.

"The United States government is advising all American citizens to leave the Orient. They can't guarantee our safety."

Imogene's gaze flew to Jimmy. A cold chill ran through her. Beneath the table Jimmy grasped her hand. For a moment neither spoke.

Then he said lightly, "Don't worry. It's just another move in the game of politics. The United States doesn't want war. And certainly Japan will never attack America."

four

The stopover in Hawaii had been brief, too brief. For in that peaceful paradise it seemed Imogene and Jimmy's fondness for one another grew more intense with each wave that washed the pristine shore. In tacit agreement, neither had spoken of Miss Yoder's announcement, protecting themselves in a cocoon spun of their devotion and dreams. But the memory of her words wafted around them as persistent as the plumeria-scented breeze.

As the *SS Calvin Coolidge* navigated out of Pearl Harbor, Imogene gazed up at the battleships looming on either side, and reality slapped her with a force that made her shudder.

Jimmy drew her close. But his embrace could not warm her chilled heart. All that Imogene had taken for granted—freedom, justice, love—seemed suddenly in jeopardy.

Gloom, dense as a coastal fog, fell on the entire ship the closer they came to Japan. And nowhere was it more evident than in the ship's dining room. It muffled the clink of cutlery and conversation and the brief, jarring spurts of unexpected laughter.

Even Raymond Diller was subdued.

"I miss Mrs. Nickleson," Miss Yoder murmured, glancing at the vacant seat. "She was a most congenial person."

Mrs. Duke agreed. "A very genteel lady." She swallowed a bite of the rich pot d'creme dessert.

"But I'm glad for her. The holidays are so much happier when spent with one's family," Miss Yoder said. "Her son is an officer on the *Arizona*, you know."

"So she said." Mrs. Duke patted her lips with the corner of her napkin. "Hawaii is lovely, but for lush, tropical beauty, there's nothing like the Philippines. By the time we get home, the servants will have the decorations up for Christmas." She sighed. "I can hardly wait."

Imogene would have been just as eager to get home had she not met Jimmy. But now, as the days moved toward that inevitable moment of their separation when they would dock in Yokohama, the thought of being apart from him, no matter how happy the homecoming, was almost unbearable.

"We still have the equator to cross," Miss Yoder reminded Mrs. Duke. "Then Hong Kong."

"And Yokohama," Raymond Diller said. "The last stop before the Philippines." He shoveled a large spoonful of dessert into his mouth. "If the U.S. government is warning us to stay out of Japan, I'll lay odds they'll be encouraging the Japs to go back where they belong—and good riddance," he added under his breath.

There was a beat of embarrassed silence and the inevitable furtive glance in Jimmy's direction.

Imogene felt her face grow hot as she struggled, once again, for self-control. *Please, God, help me to remember that "a soft answer turneth away wrath."* But as she looked at the ruddy, mean face of Raymond Diller, not one soft word came to mind.

She put down her fork. She'd lost her appetite. Even for chocolate.

"You're not touching your dessert." Mrs. Duke glanced at Imogene's bowl as she delicately scraped up the last remaining morsel from her own. "I can't say that I blame you. It doesn't compare with the pot d'creme they serve at the Ambassador

Hotel in Los Angeles."

"Chocolate pudding is chocolate pudding." Mr Diller, having polished off his own portion, was now tackling his wife's.

No wonder poor Mrs. Diller was such a thin little waif.

"I will also be disembarking in Japan," Miss Yoder said.

Jimmy leaned forward. "Where will you be staying, Miss Yoder?"

"I have a reservation in a little hotel in Yokohama the first night. The next day some friends are picking me up to take me back to the mission."

"There'll be a limousine waiting for me at the dock. You must let me drop you off at your hotel."

"If it's not too much trouble—that would be lovely."

"And if you don't have other plans, I'd be honored to have you join me and my family for dinner. My mother would especially enjoy learning about your mission."

Miss Yoder smiled. "Why, Jimmu, how kind. I would be delighted."

Clearly, the dear lady was pleased with the prospect of being invited by such a handsome, intelligent, sensitive young man to share a meal with his family.

Any woman would be.

As Imogene contemplated being invited home to meet Jimmy's parents, he suddenly turned, rewarding her with a flashing grin. "I hope you're just a little jealous," he whispered.

"Rest assured I am." She smiled back.

❧

On the night before they would reach Japan, Imogene and Jimmy sat alone on a small couch in the farthest corner of the lounge. Imogene had so much she wanted to say to him, so much she needed to hear. So little time.

Jimmy reached for her hand, lacing his fingers through

hers with a gentle, persuasive pressure. "I love you, Imogene Pennington. No matter what happens, no matter what the future holds, I want you to know that." His dark eyes burned into hers.

"Oh, Jimmy—" Emotion clogged Imogene's throat. "I—"

"I see you two, hiding behind that potted palm." Mrs. Duke's strident voice rang out across the lounge. "Come along—we need another couple to complete the third table for bridge."

By the time Imogene had collected herself enough to protest, Mrs. Duke had dragged her across the lounge and pushed her down into the empty chair opposite her son, Angier.

Jimmy strode after them, obviously not pleased.

"Don't be a bad sport, Jimmy." Mrs. Duke sat down across from a stout English gentleman, motioning Jimmy to the chair opposite his henna-haired wife. She picked up her cards. "Don't worry. You'll have plenty of time for your"— her lips pursed as she gave Imogene a disapproving glance— "good-byes."

It was well after midnight by the time the bridge game finished.

Imogene and Jimmy were finally alone.

"I still have to pack," Jimmy said as they walked down the corridor to Imogene's stateroom. "I waited until the last minute"—he gave her a rueful smile—"maybe because I was hoping the last minute would never come."

"Oh, Jimmy." Imogene blinked back tears as she felt his strong arms wrap around her. "I'm so afraid you're going to forget me."

"Impossible! How could I forget the sweetest, happiest memory of the most wonderful girl in the world?"

"Don't say just a memory, Jimmy. That sounds too final."

She leaned away from him. "We'll see each other again—we must."

"And we will, my darling girl." He hugged her to him, nestling her head in the curve of his shoulder. "I'll come to the Philippines as soon as I can."

"But when? I'm returning to the States in January."

"Then I'll find you there." Jimmy stroked her hair. "The important thing is to keep in touch. Never lose touch."

🙞

The next morning, their last, Imogene and Jimmy huddled at the rail as the ship pulled into Tokyo Bay and crept up the channel that led to Yokohama. The fog reflected their gloom.

Imogene pointed to a strange little island of concrete blocks in the middle of the bay. "What's that?"

"Fortifications," Jimmy said and turned away.

At that moment a customs boat pulled alongside. A Japanese officer in a crisp white uniform boarded.

Without ceremony, the officer demanded that all the passengers line up, and he began a brisk, methodical check of each passport, carefully comparing it to the passenger in front of him. Extra attention was given Miss Yoder, presumably because she would be disembarking. The exchange was in Japanese, the officer's voice brusque, Miss Yoder's gently pleading.

The officer shook his head. He snapped the passport back into her hand and moved to the next in line.

Imogene glanced up at Jimmy. "What did he say?" she whispered.

"He's not letting her leave the ship." Jimmy's expression betrayed nothing, but Imogene sensed his tension by the grip of his hand.

As the officer advanced up the line, with every booted

step, her foreboding increased. Now he stood in front of her.

He snatched the passport and proceeded to study her, scanning her from head to toe with an expression of belligerent disdain. Finally, apparently satisfied, he thrust the document back into her hand and turned to Jimmy.

He glanced at Jimmy's passport. "Ah, Jimmu Yamashida. Sakamoto Yamashida?"

Jimmy nodded.

The officer bowed stiffly from the waist as he immediately offered the passport.

Jimmy returned the courtesy with a perfunctory bow and stepped out of line. A short conversation in Japanese ensued.

Until now Imogene had seen Jimmy as a young man who spoke her language and shared her heart. For the first time she saw him as a Japanese.

It was as if a fist had hit her in the stomach. In that moment she knew the abyss that lay between them was an abyss wider than the ocean they'd just crossed. It was one of culture and language and, likely, even values.

The sudden realization made her feel the futility of ever trying to bridge it. How could she have been so naive as to think otherwise?

Jimmy abruptly followed the officer down the deck along the line of passengers. Another man stepped forward as he passed, the man who had accosted Jimmy on the dance floor, the one who had traded his seat for Imogene's. The man who, Imogene had come to realize, was Jimmy's bodyguard.

At the bulwark Jimmy paused. For an uncertain moment his eyes met Imogene's.

Even from that distance—across that abyss—she felt his anguish, too.

He turned then and, catching hold of the ladder, descended

down into the blunt-nosed customs boat that bobbed on the waves below.

Without a single word he was gone.

She ran to the rail and watched as the small motorboat carried him from her.

five

America has good reason to fear war with Japan, Jimmy thought as he serpentined his way through the soldiers massed on the dock at Yokohama. For all their obsequious bowing, the Japanese were crafty and cruel—and prepared.

But then what did America expect? On the one hand, they had put an embargo on oil and, on the other, sent their enemy the scrap metal to maintain their aggression against China.

There would be war, he had no doubt, and judging from his country's performance in China, it would not be pretty.

His friends from college would be in it—Harry Martin, his roommate; George Childs; Bruce McGragor, who stood next to him in glee club; the guys on the football team—Jimmy himself. It would be as if he were at war against his brothers.

The thought made him literally sick to his stomach.

He remembered his last precious glimpse of his beloved Imogene. The shock and despair he'd seen in her eyes tore at his heart.

He'd lacked the courage to level with her, admit who his father was, take his chances that she wouldn't reject him. Just as he'd lacked the courage to stand up to his father and stay in America.

But then he wouldn't have met Imogene.

He opened the limousine door. "Father." He spoke in Japanese.

"Welcome home, Jimmu."

As they exchanged courtesies, Jimmy fell easily into his

native language, even though he hadn't spoken more than a few words in so long. His father, so insistent that Jimmy speak perfect English, knew none himself.

Unlike the warm relationship Jimmy shared with his mother, that with his father had always been formal and distant. As long as Jimmy was compliant, and until now he'd had little reason to be otherwise, Sakamoto Yamashida supplied his son with all the advantages vast wealth could provide, but little of himself.

His father leaned forward and gave instructions to the limousine driver, then turned to Jimmy. "I made arrangements to have your luggage sent to the house. We will not need to wait. Your mother is most anxious to see you."

"Thank you, Father. I am anxious to see her."

"I might as well tell you at the outset. You will learn soon enough—"

Jimmy's heart lurched. "Is she all right? Is there—"

"Your mother is well. This has nothing to do with her. This has to do with you."

Not a good omen. He could feel his body tense.

"Because of my position, I have managed to obtain for you a two-week reprieve before you are to report for military service."

"What?" Jimmy stared at his father. "You never told me—"

"I saw no reason. It is mandatory. It is your obligation."

"But I thought since I was in America—"

"That you could dishonor family by avoiding your duty?"

"That is not what I meant. You know how I feel about war. We have discussed this a million times."

"A *million* times?" His father held up his hand. "A slight exaggeration. Even though the rarified lifestyle you and your mother 'endure' is due in large part to my business connections with the military, you have always denigrated my business—"

"That is not so, Father—"

"—as if you were ashamed."

The words struck hard with the truth, silencing Jimmy.

His father snorted and sat back in the plush seat of the limousine. "You should count yourself fortunate, Jimmu, that I *do* have friends in high places. Neither your mother nor you will be displeased with the assignment I have secured for you."

❧

The *SS Calvin Coolidge* remained in the port at Yokohama— ostensibly for repairs. But the two gunboats guarding the mouth of the channel made one wonder if that were the only reason. Were they, in fact, being held hostage? Their captain assured Imogene and her fellow passengers that was not the case, but his words did little to relieve anxiety.

Miserable and disillusioned over her aborted romance, Imogene remained largely in her stateroom and had most of her meals sent in. She couldn't bare the thought of facing Raymond Diller across the table or seeing the "Didn't I warn you?" expression in Mrs. Duke's eyes.

Miss Yoder was the only one she missed.

And Jimmy.

She tried to occupy her mind otherwise but with little success. She picked up some novels in the ship's library; but either she couldn't concentrate, or something she read would remind her of him. She tried to sleep but dreamed of him and woke with the pillow wet with her tears.

And to make matters worse, she was going to miss her sister's wedding.

Short of out-and-out war, she couldn't imagine how things could look grimmer.

Oh, how she wished her mother were alive. As a child she could pour out her heart, and somehow her mother always knew what to say to comfort her.

On the third day in port, she was so depressed that she didn't even bother to get dressed.

Midafternoon she heard a light tap on her stateroom door.

"It's Goldie Yoder, Imogene. Are you all right, Dear? We've missed you at dinner."

"Miss Yoder." Imogene sat up. "Just a minute." Hastily she put on her robe and smoothed the coverlet on the bed where she'd been lying. She grabbed her hairbrush from the vanity and stopped short at the face that met hers in the mirror.

Her dark hair hung lank and unattended, her red-rimmed eyes dull in her pale face. She was a truly pathetic sight.

"Imogene?"

"Just give me a minute." Even dear, understanding Miss Yoder shouldn't have to see her looking like this. She yanked her hair back into a ponytail, smudged on a bit of lipstick, and pinched her cheeks.

But the small gesture was not enough. When she opened the door, the older woman's round, baby-doll face fell at the sight of her. "My dear Imogene."

Imogene took one look at her friend's sweet expression of sincere concern and, deciding she was the next best thing to a mother, burst into tears.

For some time they sat side by side on the edge of the bed while Imogene spilled out her feelings, and Miss Yoder, her face filled with compassion, stroked Imogene's hand and made little clucking sounds of comfort and encouragement.

"I feel like such a naive fool," Imogene said, finally running out of steam.

"You shouldn't chastise yourself, my dear. Jimmy is a fine young man and, I assure you, profoundly disturbed by what is happening in his country. I talked with him at length on several occasions, and, indeed, I believe him to have all the admirable qualities you see in him. He is intelligent, talented, compassionate, and"—she smiled—"most certainly handsome. Why, any clear-eyed, young lady with good sense would be drawn to him."

Imogene leaned forward and gave the dear little woman's plump, lined cheek an impulsive kiss. "Oh, Miss Yoder, thank you. Just talking to you helps." She took her hands. "But here I am going on and on about my troubles, when your whole life has been turned upside down. Now that they won't let you back into Japan, what are you going to do?"

"I really don't know, my dear." Miss Yoder sighed, and then her expression brightened. "But I do have every confidence that the Lord knows exactly. He simply hasn't chosen to reveal it to me as yet."

Imogene squeezed her hands. "Well, until He does, you will stay with us at the plantation."

"Oh, my dear—"

"It's settled. With my sister marrying, we'll have plenty of room." Imogene's violet eyes turned dark. "Oh, Miss Yoder, even if we'd sailed yesterday, it would have been too late. I'm going to miss my sister's wedding."

The fourth day held no more promise for their departure than the day before. Imogene was truly in a state of despair when just after lunch a rather flat, square package arrived.

With trembling fingers, she tore off the brown paper wrapping.

A note lay on top of the black velvet box:

My dearest Imogene,
I never thought I could miss anyone the way I miss
you. I yearn to see your beautiful face but realize now it

*may be a very long time before I do. Whatever happens,
know that I love you. Please, dear heart, remember me,
as I will remember you—always.*

With all my love,
Jimmy

"With all my love," she repeated as she opened the hinged
jewelry box.

On the creamy satin within, three strands of blush-pink
seed pearls rested. A rose-gold pendant fashioned in the
shape of a heart was attached, and from the point in its center
hung a luminescent pearl teardrop.

The girl who was so emotional she could weep at a cereal
commercial was too stunned to cry. For some moments
Imogene could only stare down in silence at the treasure. It
would be an eternal reminder of where Jimmy held her in his
heart and the sadness he felt at their parting.

How could she have doubted him?

They would find each other again. They must.

six

Finally, on the sixth day in port, the *SS Calvin Coolidge* was given permission to sail.

Imogene stood at the rail, hoping against hope to see Jimmy running up the gangplank to join her, but the ship steamed out of Yokohama Bay without him. To make matters worse, it was her sister's wedding day. Becky would be married without her maid of honor. The letter from Jimmy, the pendant, and the love they represented served as her only consolation.

Five days later she caught her first glimpse of the gilded tips of the Horns of Negros rising above the tinted clouds, and she knew she would soon be home.

As the ship sailed into port at Dumaguete, the capital of the Philippine island of Negros, her heart swelled at the thought of seeing her father again after almost two years. She stood on deck and grasped Miss Yoder's hand, searching the crowded pier for his dear face.

"There he is. There he is." Bobbing up and down on her toes, she pointed. "He's the tall one, the one with the glasses."

Will Pennington was hard to miss. Bronzed and rangy, with the sinewy body of an outdoorsman, at six-foot-four he stood head and shoulders above everyone else on the dock. Although Imogene guessed he was Miss Yoder's contemporary, his thinning gray hair was the only clue to his sixty-five years.

"And there's Becky. She's that tall, dark-haired girl next to him—what's she doing here? She should be in Manila with

David." Imogene's excitement was momentarily tainted by concern. But then she saw the smile on her sister's face, and her heart lifted.

The first to run down the gangplank, she hurtled into her father's arms, sprinkling kisses over his craggy face. "Ooh, I love you—it's so good to see you." Then she hugged and kissed her sister with equal enthusiasm. "Where's David? I was desolate at missing the wedding. I want to hear every detail. There's so much—oh dear, I almost forgot." She rushed back and pulled Miss Yoder into the fold of her family's welcome. "This is my friend, Miss Yoder. She was supposed to disembark in Japan, but they wouldn't let her off the ship, and she had no place to go." The words all came out in one breath. "So I invited her to stay with us."

Her father's face reflected only momentary surprise. He shook his head, broke into a grin, and grasped the plump little lady's small hand in his. "Welcome to the Philippines, Miss Yoder."

Miss Yoder treated him to a dimpled smile. "Please call me Goldie. That goes for you girls, too."

Imogene gave her a hug. "Very well, from now on, Miss Goldie it will be."

"Goldie Yoder," Imogene's father mused. "What a remarkably charming name."

Breathless questions flew between the two sisters, neither taking time for answers, as their father crammed Imogene's luggage in the car's generous trunk and tucked Miss Goldie's small suitcase into the backseat.

"Will Pennington." A voice rang out behind them. Mrs. Duke swept forward on her long, sturdy legs, her hand extended. "Agatha Duke, Babcock Duke's wife. We met at the Governor's Ball two years ago. You remember my son, Angier."

Angier dipped his head, a hank of dark hair flopping over his brow. His twitching eye focused on the older man's left ear.

Imogene's father gave a slight bow over Mrs. Duke's proffered hand. "A pleasure to see you both again. This is my daughter Rebecca Spaneas and—"

"You don't have to introduce us to Imogene," the woman interrupted. "We've become great friends—"

That will be the day. .

"And, of course, I'm acquainted with Miss Yoder, too."

Angier pulled at his mother's sleeve. "I think Father's trying to get your attention."

"They must have finished loading our luggage." Agatha Duke turned back to Imogene's father. "We'll have to get together for bridge one evening. Your daughter Imogene is quite a master. I was disappointed we could never induce her to play after her partner, Jim-mu Ya-ma-shi-da"—she articulated each syllable separately—"left us in Yokohama." The woman pursed her lips into a tight smile. "Maybe you'll have better luck convincing her." With a slight wave, Mrs. Duke turned. "We'll be in touch soon. Lovely meeting you, Rebecca." And she sailed off, Angier in tow.

It was clear Mrs. Duke hoped that by mentioning Jimmy's name that she had dropped a bomb in the middle of the Pennington family.

Well, she was out of luck. Imogene's was a cosmopolitan upbringing, devoid of prejudice or cultural rancor. But still, given the state of the world, the fact that Jimmy was Japanese might cause her father a moment's pause.

He helped Miss Goldie into the front seat while Imogene and Becky squeezed into the back with Miss Goldie's luggage. And then they were off.

"So who is this Yamashida?" her father asked almost at once.

Oh, oh. Imogene stared down at her clasped hands. She could feel his gaze boring into her in the rearview mirror and Becky's curious look. "A—a friend."

"You're nose is growing, little sister," Becky whispered, her dark eyes glittering.

Imogene shot her a warning glance.

The truth was, Imogene wanted to tell her father about Jimmy, announce everything. She wanted to roll down the car window and shout to the passing palm trees and the water buffalo cooling in the mud by the side of the road and the white herons perched on their mud-covered backs and the stevedores and the villagers: "I love Jimmy Yamashida! I love him, and what's more, he loves me, and I have this to prove it." She touched the collar of her blouse, under which the heart-shaped pendant hid.

But for the first time with her beloved father, she felt shy and fearful. She'd seen how Jimmy was treated on the ship by Raymond Diller, how the Japanese customs officer had behaved toward Miss Goldie. And she realized how quick her father was to question her.

Did it make a difference to him, after all, that Jimmy was Japanese?

"Is this Jimmu Yamashida any relation to the Japanese shipbuilder by that name?" her father asked.

Imogene glanced at Miss Goldie. "So I'm told."

He frowned. "Are you aware of his father's reputation?"

"I've heard."

"Just remember—the apple doesn't fall far from the tree."

"So you always say. But you're making assumptions on someone you've never met, Daddy."

Miss Goldie cleared her throat. "If I may," she said gently, "I think Jimmy may be the exception to the rule, Mr. Pennington.

In the short time I've known him, I have found him to be a fine, Christian young man, with the highest values and principles."

"I hope you're right." Mr. Pennington veered to avoid a cart being drawn by a water buffalo meandering down the center of the road. "I suppose it's a moot point anyway. Given the present situation, I doubt Imogene will be socializing with him or any other Japanese in the foreseeable future."

"Oh, Daddy, don't say that."

"I'm on Imo's side, Daddy. There's no need to be so pessimistic. Before we make up our minds, I think we should wait until we know more about him. You don't want Miss Goldie to get the impression you're prejudiced or rush to judge."

Imogene mouthed, "Thank you," to her sister.

"Oh, I would never think so, Mr. Pennington," Miss Goldie said.

"Will, please."

"Will."

"Thank you, Miss Goldie." He cast her a bemused smile. "As you can see, if I get out of line, I can always count on my daughters to whip me back into shape."

He caught Imogene's gaze again in the rearview mirror, and she knew this was only a momentary reprieve, not an end to the discussion.

In the meantime, her father turned his attention to Miss Goldie. He pointed out places of interest, entertaining her with bits of history, as they cruised on the crushed coral road through groves of coconut palms, past lush green rice fields, and through towns shaded by acacias and flame trees.

Imogene gave Becky a sidelong look. "So you got married without your little sister to supervise."

"You have no idea how disappointed I was. David, too."

"If you'd been that disappointed, you could have cancelled

the caterers, returned the gifts, and rescheduled at a time more convenient for me."

"Oh, you." Becky gave her a fierce hug.

"Why isn't he here?"

"He wanted to wait and see you, but he had to get back early to the university. They hired two new professors from Germany—Jews. Sometimes, with the promise of a job, they're allowed to leave. The Adamsons have been able to get quite a number of teachers out that way."

"That's wonderful. But I'm surprised this once they couldn't get someone else to greet them. After all, David is still on his honeymoon."

Becky smiled. "Unfortunately, as head of the department, it's his job to orient the new faculty. Besides"—her smile broadened—"I kind of wanted to have my baby sister all to myself for a few days. I have a whole lifetime ahead of me to be with David."

Imogene was touched by a tranquility reflected in her sister's face that she'd never seen there before.

"I hope my being here is not going to create a problem," Miss Goldie said to the girls' father. "I'm sure I'd have no trouble finding other accommodations."

"We wouldn't hear of it," he said. "Becky leaves for Manila on Monday. You shall have her room, and she can share Imogene's. They'll be up all night gossiping anyway."

"I wouldn't want to put Rebecca out."

"You won't," Becky said. "I'm very glad you're here. You can keep Daddy occupied while I get the straight scoop on my baby sister's love life—and other things, of course."

"We're used to Imogene's unexpected guests," her father said, grinning into the mirror.

"We're just grateful she's brought one of the human species

home this time," Becky said. "When she was a little girl, it was usually the four-legged variety."

"Not always," Imogene said. "Remember the three-legged dog I picked up at the beach?"

"Imogene!" her father admonished, in mock horror. "You're certainly not putting our lovely guest, Miss Goldie, in the same category as a three-legged dog?"

"It's no insult, Daddy. I loved that dog." Imogene laughed and patted Miss Goldie affectionately on the shoulder.

On the beach side of the road, they were passing thatched houses on bamboo stilts, nestled among areca palms and clumps of banana trees. Closer to the water, outriggers and dugout canoes were pulled up along the sand.

"Look out there." Her father pointed at the little ferry crossing the calm, blue water of Tañon Strait toward the nearby island of Cebu.

"Beautiful." Miss Goldie sighed.

They turned inland, and their plantation spread before them in waves of green that rolled across the valley to meet the jungle-covered mountain.

It was Saturday, December 6, 1941, and Imogene was home at last.

Hibiscus, large yellow bells in full bloom, and bougainvillea banked the house and splashed onto the freshly mowed lawn. As the car pulled into the *silong,* the space beneath the ground and the first floor, the servant girls, Bertha and Lupe, ran down the front stairs to greet Imogene. The three exchanged warm hugs while her father and Pedro, the plantation foreman, collected the luggage.

Imogene was relieved to see that the white orchids still blossomed in profusion along the open gallery that led to the kitchen and that Caruso, her canary, still warbled his welcome from the large screen cage.

Upstairs it seemed nothing had changed. The Philippine mahogany walls and floor were burnished to a dull luster, and a soft breeze carried its fragrance through the latticed airspace between the top of the wall and the roof's thatch.

She tossed her hat into the peacock chair and danced around the room breathing in the perfumed air. "It's so good to be home." Grabbing Becky's hand, she pulled her down the hall. "Come on—while I unpack, you can tell me every detail of the wedding."

The rest of the afternoon Becky spent curled up on the four-poster bed in Imogene's bright yellow, flowered-chintz room doing just that. "I'll send you the pictures when they've been developed," Becky said.

Imogene finished folding a white cotton sweater and tucked it into the drawer. "I can hardly wait to see them."

"I saved you some wedding cake, but I'm afraid it's pretty dried out by now." Becky stretched, adjusting the pillow at the small of her back. "Now it's your turn," she said and segued into a skill she'd spent their youth perfecting, squeezing out the secrets closest to her younger sister's heart. "So what about this Jimmu Yamashida?"

It didn't take much squeezing. Imogene was eager to spill it all, from their first meeting to the pendant at her throat.

∞

Five o'clock Monday morning, Imogene stood in the drive in her bathrobe watching as Becky and her father left for Dumaguete, where her sister would board the ship to Manila and her new husband, David. In the gray light of morning, the last thing she saw as the car disappeared around the curve was her sister's languid wave out the passenger window.

A sadness filled her heart for the precious days too quickly past. Yet for those few fleeting hours, she and Becky had been able to pretend they were still girls, young, a little foolish, without cares or responsibilities. She knew it would never be the same again. Her sister had a new life, with a new husband to go to.

As she turned back to the house, she wondered when the day would come when she would go to Jimmy.

seven

It was close to noon. The sun was bright overhead and the air thick with the sweet scent of coconut drying in the nearby copra dryer. Her father would be back soon from Dumaguete. In the meantime, Imogene had left Miss Goldie reading on the veranda and wandered alone into the garden.

In the dappled shade of a banyan tree, she sat with her legs tucked under her, vaguely aware of bees droning in the nearby hive and birds chattering in the branches above. She pulled Jimmy's note from the pocket of her pink cotton shift.

Smoothing the envelope that bore Japanese calligraphy, she caressed with her fingers where his had touched. She lifted the textured paper, imagining that the musky scent of his aftershave still lingered. How she longed to see him, to be in his arms as her sister would soon be in the arms of the man she loved.

Oh, she did envy Becky that.

Casting her gaze northward, her eyes grew moist.

How could her father, anyone, hold Jimmy responsible for the atrocities a continent away? He'd been a college student in California, as far from the chaos as it was possible to be. Yet so many did treat him as if he'd had a part in it. People like Raymond Diller painted every Japanese with the same brush.

But was it possible to be born into a culture and not be tainted by it?

Not her Jimmy. He was the dearest, kindest person she had

ever met and as American as she in his attitudes.

And yet the thought hovered in the back of her mind. Despite Jimmy's assurances to her that Japan would never risk the repercussions of attacking an American territory, did he really believe it? Or was he trying to convince himself?

As she reread his note, she realized there was something haunting, almost final in his last words: "Please, dear heart, remember me, as I will remember you—always."

The flickering shadow of a bending palm fell across the page. It reminded her of Hawaii and Jimmy's arms around her as they watched the palms along the shore swaying in another soft, tropical breeze.

Imogene blinked. The shadow on the page had taken on a human silhouette. She looked up and through the glitter of tears saw her father standing above her.

His expression was dazed, as if he couldn't quite accept what he was about to say. "The Japanese have attacked the American ships at Pearl Harbor."

"No, they didn't." A mantle of fear dropped over her. "They wouldn't." She tried to swallow but couldn't get past the lump in her throat. Barely could she draw a breath.

"We heard the news when we got to Dumaguete. And that's not the worst of it. Bombs are falling on our own capital—on Manila—as we speak."

His voice, usually so strong and confident, wavered with uncertainty. His tall, imposing frame was stooped, as if the weight of his words hung like a yoke around his neck. And his ruddy, sun-baked face was pinched and drawn.

For the first time Imogene saw him as old.

How arrogant she had been in her innocence. She clutched Jimmy's letter to her heart. "This means—"

"We're at war."

eight

Imogene rose. Her legs trembled so she had to catch herself on her father's arm. "Becky? She came back with you?"

"She went straight to the house," he murmured, too wretched to meet Imogene's eyes. "I'm worried about her, Imogene. She didn't say a word on the way home."

"She must be terrified for David. Oh, Daddy, what are we going to do?" Imogene clung to her father, counting on his strength as she had as a child, and realized for the first time in her life that he couldn't protect her.

"God will protect us," he said, as if he had read her thoughts. "The Bible says, 'Our soul waiteth for the Lord: He is our help and our shield.' I believe that, Imogene."

She only hoped her father was right. At the moment God seemed very far away.

Miss Goldie met them at the door, her sweet face creased with concern. "Rebecca's in your room. Go to her, Imogene; she won't talk to me."

Without knocking, Imogene burst into her bedroom.

Becky was stretched out on the bed; her long, dark hair, usually caught in a French twist, lay in a tangled mass on the pillow. Unlike Imogene who had the rounded curves of their mother who had died, Becky was their father's child, lean and tall with the strong, assertive body of an athlete. But now her body seemed diminished and melted listlessly into the comforter. Despite the red rimming her soft brown eyes, she had no tears as she stared with an inward gaze at the ceiling above her.

If she'd heard Imogene enter, she did not respond.

Imogene rushed over and kneeled beside the bed. She grasped Becky's limp hand in both of hers. "Oh, Becky, please look at me. Speak to me."

Becky turned her head slowly. Gradually her eyes focused on Imogene. "What is there to say?"

"You're worried about David. I know that's it. But he'll be all right. I'm sure he will. He's so smart—he'll know where to go to be safe."

Becky turned away. She closed her eyes, and the first tear dribbled down her cheek. "If he's dead, I want to be dead, too," she whispered.

"You mustn't say that." Frantically Imogene clutched Becky's hand. She'd never seen her older sister like this. It was so out of character. Becky, the take-charge one. The strong one. "You can't mean it."

"How could you understand, little sister? You're only twenty. What do you know about loving someone enough to give up everything for him, to trust him with your life?" Becky rolled over on her side, away from Imogene, and began to sob. "To want to die without him."

Could Imogene love someone that much?

She put her hand in the pocket of her shift where she'd shoved Jimmy's note.

Before that horrifying moment when her father had pronounced the dreaded word *war,* before this hollowness where her heart had been and this panic wrenching inside her, her answer would have come easily. Yes. She could love someone that much.

Now she was not sure.

In this new anguish and fear, the trip back from America seemed a dream. Jimmy seemed a dream. But he wasn't. Her hand left the letter in her pocket and found its way to the heart pendant. Jimmy's gift of love. A love as real and as true as Becky's. It was!

"Imogene. Rebecca." Their father stood in the open door. "We must act immediately." The strength had returned to his voice and his stance. "Come into the living room. We need to talk."

Miss Goldie, now considered one of them in this moment of crisis, sat in the rocker in the corner. The girls' father entered the room and settled into the peacock chair. Imogene perched anxiously on the love seat beneath the window, her despondent sister beside her.

"Miss Goldie and I have been talking," he began. "We think it prudent for each of us to pack one bag, in case it's necessary to leave in a hurry. We'll also have Bertha and Lupe prepare some small containers of staples and a few essentials, light enough for each of us to carry. We need medical supplies, quinine for malaria, a snakebite kit—"

"Bug repellent," Imogene added.

"Naturally. I'll take care of all that. In the meantime, I'm sending Pedro to prepare a campsite in the jungle up beyond the mill road, in case we need it."

He leaned forward. "The important thing is to keep a balanced attitude. Bear in mind that these are just precautions. I stopped by Major Hirsch's office as we were leaving Dumaguete. He said he expects help to come from the States within the month. He assures me his men can hold out until then." His gaze swept the silent group in front of him. "Any questions?"

Too dazed to put their thoughts or feelings into words, Imogene and the others glanced at each other briefly and looked away, as if they were embarrassed that they could think of nothing to say.

All but Miss Goldie. Her small hands were folded over the Bible in her lap. "There's a passage in Psalms I'd like to share, if I may."

"Please, Miss Goldie," Imogene's father said.

She opened the well-worn book, thumbing through the pages until she found the verses she sought. "It is Psalm 46: 'God is our refuge and strength, a very present help in trouble. Therefore will not we fear, though the earth be removed, and though the mountains be carried into the midst of the sea.' And then further on, 'He maketh wars to cease unto the end of the earth; he breaketh the bow, and cutteth the spear in sunder; he burneth the chariot in the fire. Be still, and know that I am God.'"

For several minutes they remained silent. Miss Goldie, in her gentle way, had reminded them of the source of their strength and refuge.

Imogene studied her sister's face and that of her father and saw the comfort they'd derived from hearing those profound words. She wished it were the same for her. In the face of everything that was happening, she couldn't feel that certain.

❧

For the next two months, they tried to maintain at least a pretense of normalcy, but it was almost impossible.

There were landings on the islands to the north and south of theirs. Enemy airplanes roared in formation overhead, and enemy ships were sighted along the coast. The stores were rapidly emptying of food supplies.

Will Pennington buried their important documents in a metal drum out behind the copra dryer.

Imogene's heart nearly broke at the pitiful sight of the native families passing through their plantation, less frightened of the malarial foothills than the advancing enemy.

Everyone remembered the rape of Nanking and the harsh occupation of Indochina.

A radiogram from her college roommate, Daisy, offered a momentary respite.

> *Dearest friend abandons me, then brother Court*
> *shipped overseas. Boys at Oxy are signing up in droves.*
> *Even Ted. College looks like a girls' school. Who will*
> *take me to the senior prom?*

But they had no word from Becky's David.

The new bride was sick with worry, literally, constantly nauseated, unable to keep a meal down. The robust one hundred thirty-five pounds on her five-foot-eight-inch frame shrank by ten pounds in just two weeks. Even Miss Goldie's efforts to concoct appealing delicacies failed to tempt her.

It was about this time Becky realized she was pregnant.

"What will I do without David?" she cried, distraught.

"Don't be afraid, Becky. By the time this baby arrives, the Americans will have come back, and you'll be safe with David." Imogene knew her words were hollow, but what else could she say?

Frightened as they were, they found solace in their faith. Will Pennington had brought up his daughters so their religion was a daily measure, not just a last resort in times of trouble. For Miss Goldie, it was her life. Even when things looked darkest, some of that "peace that passeth understanding" seemed to be there. Imogene struggled.

The news on the radio intensified their fears as Hong Kong fell, then Manila, Zamboanga, Batavia, Rangoon, Singapore, Bataan, and Cebu, just across the Tañon Strait—within sight of the shores of Negros.

When the last remaining soldiers were forced to surrender, Corregidor fell, and so did their last hope. It was only a matter of time before Negros would be taken, too.

The Pennington household left early the following morning, with little in hand.

"When we're gone, I want you all to take away everything you can carry," Imogene's father instructed the weeping servants.

"Better they should have it than the Japanese," Imogene overheard him confide to Miss Goldie. "In all likelihood, the house will be looted and burned to the ground."

Her heart went sick with sadness.

Her father, who had engineered many of the island's roads and was familiar with the terrain, led the way. Imogene, Miss Goldie, and Becky followed, each bearing a suitcase with her own clothing and a small bundle of either provisions or medical supplies.

As they trudged up the road and rounded the first curve that led up to the old mill, Imogene turned for one last look at the only home she had known since birth.

A wrenching bitterness gripped her. Against the enemy. Against God. If He was their refuge and strength, how could He have allowed this to happen?

Bertha and Lupe stood in a patch of sun on the lawn, waving, tears streaming down their cheeks.

They were more than servants; Imogene and her sister had grown up with them, been playmates since childhood. She set down her suitcase and lifted her hand in response and wondered if she would ever see their dear, sweet faces again.

On such a bright, sunny day, it was hard to believe the darkness rapidly descending over them all.

In the beginning the climb was not too difficult. The trees soared to a height of almost a hundred feet, allowing scant foliage in the perpetual twilight of the jungle floor. But it became more unpleasant as they went along, forging through creeks, backtracking so as to leave no trace. Snakes slithered across their path, and the insects were bold, but no bolder or as feared as the enemy from which they fled.

After a day and a half, they reached a small clearing.

"Our estate," Imogene's father said.

In the center was a long, one-room structure that was to be their home. Their foreman, Pedro, and his sons had constructed it without nails, of only the materials at hand. The floor was of split trunks, lashed to supporting rattan poles, the roof of overlapping palm leaves, shaggy from the outside but smooth and neat within.

"No bathroom?" Imogene said.

Becky managed a small smile and pointed at a large tree a few steps deeper into the jungle. "Over there."

At that moment a brief, torrential rain, one of many they endured in that tropical climate, caused them to scurry for cover.

"With a flush toilet," Imogene observed, dropping her suitcase onto the rough floor. "All the comforts of home." And then she laughed out loud. "If only Daisy could see me now. This is certainly a far cry from Oxy and our lovely room in Erdmen Hall that overlooks the rose garden."

They became used to bathing and washing their clothes in the stinging cold water of the creek and cooking on the tiny earthenware stove they had brought. They amused themselves with cards. And they found comfort in the Bible. "Yea, though I walk through the valley of the shadow of death, I will fear no evil. . .Thy rod and Thy staff they comfort me."

They managed to keep the bugs and the snakes at bay, but never the fear that one day the Japanese would find them.

Survival, physical and mental, occupied their days. But nights were hardest, when Imogene couldn't conquer her mind. When she dreamed of Jimmy—dreams of what was and what might have been—and was awakened by the soft muted sobs of Becky on the cot beside her.

nine

Imogene listened to the soft snores of her father melding with the night sounds of the jungle, the random squawks and whistles, the rustle of leaves as a wild hog passed through into the clearing, a cracking branch. The whoosh of a bat's wings. She listened with ears sharpened by familiarity.

Suddenly she sat upright, her heart beating furiously against her chest.

There was a different sound tonight. More leaves rustling. More twigs breaking.

Was that a pinpoint of light?

Gone.

Yes, there it was again.

She reached over and shook her sister on the shoulder. "Wake up, Becky," she whispered.

As if that were the signal, lights suddenly flashed on.

A cacophony of shouting voices filled the night air.

Numb with fear, Imogene scrambled to her knees as Becky and Miss Goldie sat upright, blinking in the bright lights flooding the interior.

She heard a scuffle and turned to see a Japanese soldier grab her father and pin back his arms.

"Daddy!" she screamed.

Miss Goldie jumped up and ran across the room, pushing the soldier away as she shouted at him in Japanese.

This was a new Miss Goldie, bold and passionate as a mother lion, protecting her cubs.

The young soldier was so surprised at the little dervish dashing at him that he stepped back, releasing the older man.

A second soldier, apparently the one in charge, tromped across the floor and confronted her. But she was unmoved. The sturdy little lady stood her ground and looked up at him, her curly head bobbing as she gestured and articulated in Japanese, her voice as harsh and dissonant as his.

With a final word he marched down the steps, gesturing the other soldier to follow.

Miss Goldie let out a protracted sigh.

Imogene could see that for all her bravery, she was trembling.

"The lieutenant says we are to dress. We may carry one suitcase each. We will leave in ten minutes."

And so they did, abandoning the encroaching jungle, the monkeys, the birds, and the wild boar, their home for the last three months.

Stumbling out of the camp, Imogene's thoughts were as dark with foreboding as the night that enshrouded them.

In the ensuing days, her fears were not allayed. Without sleep or food and scant water, she and her family struggled back through the jungle, pushed, prodded, and harangued at by their captors. No mercy was given, even to the obviously pregnant Becky. It was as if, in their cruelty, they reveled in her misery.

When the Penningtons reached Tanjay, they were transported by truck to the provincial headquarters in Dumaguete. There they were ordered to the infamous Santo Tomás prison camp on the outskirts of Manila. But out of those grim tidings rose hope. At last Becky would be able to find out about her husband, David.

Like cattle being led to the slaughter, the family was herded onto a filthy barge, its deck thick with crude oil, its public sanitary facilities three terrifyingly large holes over the water at the boat's stern. For five days they drank contaminated water and shared food given them by other kind prisoners, almost as destitute as they.

More amazing to Imogene than the fact that they had all survived thus far was the fact that Miss Goldie and her father, even Becky, still continued to believe they were in God's hands and that He was their hope and refuge.

At least it gave them solace. Imogene wished she could be as optimistic.

Sick with dysentery and dehydration, their faces blistered from the sun, smelling as rank as the foul tub in which they'd sailed, Imogene, Becky, their father, and Miss Goldie disembarked in Manila for the last leg of their journey through the subdued streets of this once-bustling city.

As their bus drove through the gates of the walled internment camp, Imogene's father mused, "To think, Santo Tomás was once the oldest university under the American flag."

"What a pity it has to come to this," Miss Goldie said sadly.

Imogene looked out the smudged window. Canvas chairs were scattered across the campus lawn and grouped under the acacia trees. Internees, roaming freely within the confines of the campus walls, swarmed around the bus, curious about the newcomers. They looked cheerful and reasonably well fed. Maybe it wasn't going to be that bad, after all. But seeing so many Americans held captive was unsettling.

The bus pulled up to the main office, where one of the camp's elected officials assigned living accommodations to the family and the hour of their interview appointment with the commandant.

According to Japanese instructions, the sexes were separated, even if they were married. In this case Imogene, Becky, and Miss Goldie were quartered in a dorm, the girls' father in the gymnasium.

"Just think of it as a Boy Scout jamboree," Imogene said sardonically to her father.

Imogene, Becky, and Miss Goldie stood inside the doorway of the small dorm room to which they'd been assigned. In a room intended for two beds, seven cots had been squeezed in. There were four on the side facing the door, three opposite, leaving just enough room in the middle for a narrow aisle.

Becky leaned wearily against the doorjamb. "So much for privacy."

"What did you expect, the Ritz?" A heavyset girl with a pouty expression and straight blond ponytail looked up from the movie magazine she was reading.

Miss Goldie managed a small, conciliatory smile toward the room's occupant and turned back to Becky. "I wouldn't complain, Rebecca dear. Compared to our last accommodations, this *seems* like the Ritz."

"I'm Cluny Baxter, the room monitor." The girl's feet clunked to the floor, and she rose to an impressive height of almost six feet. "Those are available." She pointed to the three cots along the near wall. "Store your belongings under your beds, and I recommend you keep anything of value on your person. There are some sticky fingers in this place."

Imogene touched the pendant. No problem there. They'd have to chop off her head to get it.

"I could use a shower," Becky said, dropping her suitcase onto the bed in the corner.

"With eight hundred women on this floor—"

"Eight hundred?" The number stunned Imogene.

"That's right. Each room is assigned a specific time for the showers. But in your case"—Cluny wrinkled her nose and delicately squeezed its tip—"I think we can make an exception."

≥◆

An hour later, somewhat revived by a shower and a change of clothes, the family reconnoitered outside camp headquarters for their appointed interviews. They were to be summoned in alphabetical order, which meant Miss Goldie would come after the Penningtons.

"Keep your eyes lowered when you enter the office," she instructed when their name was called. "And don't worry if the officer who conducts the interview doesn't look at you. That's considered Japanese etiquette."

But, despite Miss Goldie's warning, Imogene sneaked a look.

In that brief moment she caught an impression of a large, clean-shaven head with a coarse-featured face and narrow, speculative eyes, all set on a barrel-shaped torso. Quickly she lowered her gaze. Contrary to the Japanese etiquette, however, she felt the heat of the man's direct and bold assessment of her.

He spoke in Japanese, his voice guttural and dissonant.

She shuddered at the sound.

An interpreter at the desk to his right translated. "The commandant wishes me to warn you that he understands English." The man spoke impeccably, without the trace of a Japanese accent—and in a distinctly familiar voice.

ten

Jimmy absently straightened the forms on his desk. As the commandant's interpreter, he automatically repeated his usual sentence, warning the new American internees that the commandant understood English.

He glanced up.

It was as if a fist had hit him in the chest.

It wasn't possible. Imogene here at Santo Tomás?

He couldn't believe it. He expected she would be interned in Dumaguete or Bacolod on Negros, not here, in Manila.

Panic gripped him. *Dear God, don't let her react.* It would not be safe if the commandant suspected anything between them.

His beloved Imogene. He couldn't keep his eyes off her. How thin she looked, her golden skin scorched painfully by the sun, her shoulders stooped. Still, she was beautiful. His heart was sick. He wanted to go to her, draw her into his arms, comfort her, kiss away the sadness he saw in her face.

Next to her stood a haggard-looking older man and a pregnant, dark-haired young woman. They must be her sister and her father.

The commandant leaned forward, elbows on his desk. His eyes narrowed as he assessed Imogene with lingering satisfaction. He moistened his lips.

Jimmy broke the pencil in half that he was holding. A white rage nearly blinded him. He had an almost uncontrollable urge to jump up and grab the man by the throat.

How dare he desecrate this precious, virginal woman with such obvious intent.

Lay one hand on her, and I'll rip your heart out.

The commandant looked at him curiously.

Did his emotions show that much? For all their sakes he'd better get himself under control. He returned a tight smile. "We will begin then. Please take a seat."

❧

Imogene dropped into one of the chairs in front of the commandant's desk and lowered her gaze.

Not Jimmy. Not in a Japanese uniform. It couldn't be Jimmy sitting beside the commandant.

"Please state your name for the record." But that voice. His voice.

She lifted her eyes again.

No shadow of response. No blink of his eye or twitch of his lips gave any sign of recognition.

She felt light-headed, weak. The room seemed to spin around her. She clenched her hands in her lap, her nails biting into her palms.

Breathe. In. Out. In. Out. Focus. Concentrate.

Far away her father's voice, gently demanding, "Imogene, are you all right?"

"Yes. Yes, Daddy, I'm all right."

"We will continue then," Jimmy said, his voice flat as he droned on. How much money did they bring with them? When was Mr. Pennington the provincial governor of Negros? Where on the island was his plantation? Did he know of any other Americans that might still be in hiding—

Do you honestly think he would tell you?

Imogene sat in stiff silence.

Her eyes stung; her throat was dry. But she would not give

in. Not a quiver of her lip or a tremble in her voice. She would never let him know he had just broken her heart. Never!

She had conjured a man of strength and integrity, a Christian man of conscience, of values. She had dreamed him up. For surely this cold, unfeeling Japanese soldier was not, could never be, a man she would love.

Six months it had been since she had seen him. Six months that seemed like yesterday, his face so intimately remembered. Six months that seemed a lifetime past.

He was one of them now. One of the brutal race that pillaged and tortured and raped. He wore their uniform. Oh, dear God.

"Do you have any valuables to declare?"

So you can steal them?

"No," her father said.

Becky shook her head.

"I have this." Imogene ripped at the pendant she'd taken such care to conceal beneath her blouse. Ripped with such force, the strand from which it hung broke, and pearls shot like shimmering white bullets about the room.

There was a moment of stunned silence.

Her father slipped to his knees, helping Becky scoop up the scattered beads.

It was degrading. She couldn't let them. "I'll do it," Imogene muttered.

๛

Jimmy watched mesmerized as the pearls split and scattered.

Follow the bouncing bead. But no music played in the background; no words were written beneath. The stunned silence was broken only by the clacking of the pearls dancing on the gleaming floor.

All this time she's been wearing the pendant.

"An envelope," the commandant said.

Like an automaton Jimmy obeyed, pulling an envelope from the desk, his eyes never leaving Imogene as she crouched on the floor gathering up the costly beads.

She rose and walked to the desk. Without meeting his gaze, she allowed the pearls to slide through her fingers and then the pendant.

Desolation and contempt fell over him, for himself, for his countrymen who would stand by and allow such sadness, such suffering as he saw on the faces of his beloved Imogene and her family.

He had tried to remove himself mentally, going through the motions without getting involved. He had tried not to look at the faces filled with fear, at the bodies bowed with the weight of their hopelessness and grief. But he couldn't help himself. He looked and was filled with compassion.

He'd found himself of little use as the buffer between them and the commandant, a crude, brutal man. If Jimmy even suggested the least charity, the commandant's reprimand was to take it out on the poor souls in front of them. For their sakes Jimmy soon learned to temper his compassion. He hated this war. He felt no loyalty to his country. He felt only shame.

"Mikimoto pearl?" the commandant asked.

"The commandant wishes to know the value," Jimmy said.

❧

Imogene lifted her head and stared directly into Jimmy's eyes. She kept her gaze cold and dispassionate, matching his. "None. They are no longer of any value to me."

"But they belong to you," Jimmy said quietly, extending the envelope.

"Keep them." She turned, and with all the dignity her weary

body could muster, she walked back to her chair.

Becky leaned forward, a frown troubling her brow. "Imo, why?" she whispered.

Imogene shook her head sharply.

Jimmy put down the envelope. He cleared his throat, picked up a sheet of paper from his desk, and began reading. "You will abide by the following rules. You will bow when you enter a room and when you leave it. You will bow whenever you encounter a Japanese soldier." He glanced up. "It is a serious offense not to acknowledge the emperor's representatives."

He continued. "You will attend roll call in the morning and at night and any other time deemed necessary. You will be provided two meals a day. And finally"—he put down the sheet—"any attempt to escape is"—his voice lowered—"punishable by death."

No surprise. It was war after all. But to hear the words, so callous, coming from the lips of the man she'd once loved—thought she loved. A soft moan escaped.

The commandant glanced at her. Jimmy's face remained impassive as he stared down at the sheet. After a moment he said, "The commandant wishes to know if you have any questions."

Imogene's father shifted in his chair. "There is one. My daughter Rebecca is married to David Spaneas. Have you detained him? He's a professor at Adamson University."

Jimmy riffled through a raft of papers on his desk. After a moment he looked up and shook his head. "No."

"Would it be possible—"

The commandant slammed his fist on the desk.

"The commandant wishes me to tell you he regrets there is nothing we can do." Jimmy paused. "If you have no more questions—" He rang a bell on his desk, and the soldier who had ushered them into the room reappeared.

The three stood.

Before they had taken a step, the commandant barked, "You bow!"

Stiffly they complied, retreated to the door, and bowed again.

Never let it be said that they disrespected the emperor.

It was as if they were stepping from one nightmare into another. Outside Imogene looked around at the once beautiful campus of Santo Tomás University crowded with milling groups of internees, mostly American, some Filipinos, Spanish, Chinese. All shabbily dressed. There was something surreal and sinister in the school's present incarnation.

Her father squeezed her hand. "It will be all right, Imogene. Don't worry."

She looked over at Becky and saw the tears coursing down her sister's cheeks. She felt ashamed. Here she'd been focusing on her own torment when it was nothing compared to Becky's.

Miss Goldie hurried over and did what Imogene should have done—gathered Becky into her arms. The three stood together, her father, his hand resting on Miss Goldie's shoulder, Miss Goldie comforting Becky.

Looking at them, Imogene felt like an outsider, bereft and alone and guilty for not thinking first of those who loved and needed her.

eleven

Miss Goldie was called into the office before Imogene had a chance to warn her about Jimmy. How would Jimmy react to her? Would he give her some sign of recognition, let her know in some small, subtle way that he knew her, that she still mattered to him? If he did, Miss Goldie would be luckier than Imogene.

The family waited for her in the shade of a nearby acacia. Imogene leaned back against the tree's trunk and rested a comforting hand on her sister's shoulder. Becky had managed to control her tears, but every so often a small sob escaped.

Her father stroked her arm. "You must have faith, Becky. The Lord will direct us toward the resources we need to find David. Remember—He is our hope and our salvation. Hold that in your heart."

"Daddy's right, Becky." Imogene smoothed back a strand of hair that had fallen across her sister's cheek. "We'll find David. I know we will." This was not the first time Imogene had used bold words to comfort her sister. Not the first time she had prayed her words would be true. But it was getting harder and harder to do that. To pray. Prayer was as much a part of her family's sustenance as the air they breathed and the food they consumed. Daily chapel was even required at her college.

And then the war had come.

And now it seemed that the harder she prayed, the worse things got.

As she hugged her sister, she struggled to suppress her own mix of emotions: confusion, hurt, anger, sorrow, emptiness, even chagrin. But suppress it she must, for Becky's sake. And yet she longed to let it out, to rail at the world. To shake her fist at this all-powerful, all-loving God who had allowed it to happen.

Miss Goldie was back. "It wasn't as bad as I expected," she said. "In fact, when I explained that I'd been a missionary in Japan, they treated me quite civilly."

Imogene was about to speak when she saw Miss Goldie give an almost imperceptible shake of her head. Her eyes held an implicit warning to silence.

As they walked back across the campus toward their dorm, Miss Goldie hung back and fell into step with Imogene. She laced her arm through Imogene's and leaned close, so as not to be overheard. "Jimmy did not look well, not at all well. Quite miserable, in fact."

"You must be more intuitive than I, Miss Goldie, to see misery," Imogene said rather sharply. "It appeared to me his job was to mete out misery, not to feel it."

"I doubt things are quite as they seem, my dear. Jimmy is in an almost untenable position."

"I'm sure. No doubt underneath that Japanese uniform is the same sweet boy we knew and loved. Now I suppose you're going to give me that old saw about how a leopard can't change his spots overnight." Imogene stopped suddenly and looked down at her sweet friend. "I'm sorry, Miss Goldie. I don't mean to take it out on you. But it was so awful in there, so awful—"

"Shh. Shh." Miss Goldie squeezed her hand. She glanced around with an expression of concern. Quietly she said, "I think it prudent not to let anyone know about your connection with Jimmy, Imogene. For your sake as well as his. My sense is that it could be very dangerous."

Suddenly a strident, familiar voice rang out across the crowded campus. "Imogene Pennington, is that you?" Sailing toward them came Mrs. Duke and behind her, the sallow replica, her son, Angier.

"Oh, no," Imogene muttered. "Well, it looks like the secret will be out for sure now."

"And Miss Yoder, I declare. I wondered if we'd ever see you folks again."

Mrs. Duke was as impeccably groomed as she'd been on the ship, her hair pulled into a knot at the nape of her neck, her pearl choker, her beige belted sheath. But on closer inspection Imogene could see the fray at her collar, the tiny patch on the skirt. Still, she held herself with the same imperious air, undaunted by circumstances. One had to admire her for that.

Mrs. Duke shook her head. "Isn't this the saddest reunion? At least my husband, Babcock, got out. He left on a PT boat for Mindanao with President Quezon. Angier and I were scheduled to follow, but"—she sighed—"it was too late."

"I'm so sorry," Imogene said.

"Indeed," Miss Goldie echoed.

"I received word through the Red Cross that he had arrived safely in Australia."

"Praise be to God for that," Miss Goldie said.

"Where's your father, Imogene? Oh, there he is—Will! Will Pennington!" Mrs. Duke waved.

Imogene sensed reluctance from her father, who was always the gentleman, as he and Becky returned.

"Mrs. Duke. Angier," he greeted them.

"You must have just arrived," Mrs. Duke said. "Angie's always one of the first to know what's going on here at the camp and keeps his mother apprised. Don't you, my dear?"

Angier's tight lips twitched into a modest smile.

"If there's anything you want to find out, just ask him."

"That's good to remember," Imogene's father said.

Mrs. Duke scrutinized Becky's protruding tummy. "My goodness, when we met, I didn't realize you were pregnant."

"Nor did I." Becky gave her a wan smile. "But that was six months ago."

"So it was. I can hardly believe it—so much has happened." Abruptly Mrs. Duke turned her attention to Imogene. "I imagine you were rather surprised to see your *inamorato*, Jimmu Yamashida."

Will Pennington looked at his daughter. "That young Japanese interpreter was—"

Imogene could feel the flush rising in her cheeks.

"Oh, gracious." Mrs. Duke covered her lips. "Have I let the cat out of the bag?" If she had, she didn't appear to regret it.

Imogene had disliked the woman before, but now even more so. She was a nosy busybody, and it wouldn't have surprised Imogene in the least if Babcock Duke had planned his escape to elude his wife as much as the Japanese.

"My goodness, Mrs. Duke." Imogene laughed. "I'm afraid you took my shipboard romance far more seriously than I did."

Mrs. Duke's smile was dubious. "I'm relieved to hear that, my dear. Such a relationship could have unpleasant repercussions under the circumstances. Of course you can count on us not to mention it." She turned to her son. "Can't she, Angie?"

Angier nodded brusquely and winked at Imogene.

Imogene had forgotten his nervous tick. "I must admit, though, that it was quite a surprise to see Jimmy here," she added.

"I'm afraid you'll have to get used to it. He's at every roll call and makes all the announcements that come down from the commandant's office. I must say in his defense that so far he's been very courteous. Not like some of those Japs."

Imogene cringed. Pejorative words for a race, even the Japanese, made her seethe, but she swallowed her retort. Mrs. Duke had echoed Miss Goldie's sentiments about the importance of keeping quiet about her former relationship with Jimmy. That would only be possible if she kept Mrs. Duke and Angier quiet. It was best to stay on the woman's good side, no matter how it pained her.

"Where are your rooms?" Mrs. Duke asked.

"Daddy's in the gym," Becky said, "and the three of us girls"—she smiled at Miss Goldie—"are in Franklin Hall."

"You're lucky. You have indoor plumbing. I'm in the main building. Crowded to the gills. We have to use the outside facilities. Most inconvenient."

They hadn't had many blessings lately, but an indoor bathroom was certainly one of them.

As they resumed walking, Mrs. Duke and Angier joined them. "Over there are the shanties. They're enjoyed during the day. After curfew, of course, the men and women are restricted to their separate dorms." She pointed to a grove of thatch and bamboo shacks, open on one side, the other largely of windows. "Angie and I are lucky enough to have one."

"You're fortunate." Imogene was not about to discuss her family's financial plight with Mrs. Duke, of how they had to leave everything behind and escape to the jungle.

"Yes, we have privacy. A better class of people, especially at mealtime. You want to avoid the eating sheds. They're crowded, noisy, and smelly." She wrinkled her nose. "Of course some folks put up card tables in the corridors. That helps, but there's just so much room. A shanty is much more desirable, and we can do a little cooking for ourselves."

"We were told two meals were provided," Imogene's father said.

"Breakfast is rice gruel and weak, tepid coffee. If that's what you like." She shrugged. "As for dinner, don't believe the menu they post. They may call it by different names, but it all boils—and I do mean boils—down to ground meat—one wonders the source—and greens and rice." Mrs. Duke glanced at Imogene. "It makes me long for the Fonds d'Artichauts au Caviar we had on the ship. Even if they weren't as good as Romanoff's." The bit of self-deprecating humor, for an instant, made her almost likable.

"Those of us who can afford to, buy fruit and vegetables, meat, eggs, whatever, from the camp market. Even toiletries and medicine are available. Babcock might have jumped ship, so to speak, but he left us well provided for, at least."

Ah, the truth will out. Mr. Duke's purpose might well have been to escape more than the Japanese in leaving his wife behind.

She pointed to their right. "That's the kitchen."

Angier, who'd been following obediently behind his mother, turned to Imogene. "At night there's entertainment in the plaza in front of the main building. I'd be happy to escort you. Introduce you around. Show you the ropes." As he spoke, his eyes skittered about, not quite meeting hers. Strands of lank, dark hair swagged across his forehead in the style used by men to hide their impending baldness. When he finished speaking, his mouth twitched into a smile.

"That's kind, Angier, but let me get settled first," Imogene said.

"And they have classes," he continued, as if now that he'd

gained the courage to address her, nothing was going to stop him. "French classes, Spanish classes, art, history. I myself am in the chorus. Perhaps I could interest you in that?" His mouth jerked into the now familiar smile. And he winked.

"My, Angier, with all the activities it sounds very much like summer camp."

"We try to keep occupied," he said.

By now they had reached their dorm and paused outside the entry.

"Oh, I almost forgot," Mrs. Duke said. "Remember Denice Diller?"

"Yes," Imogene said.

Miss Goldie nodded.

"You'll be running into her. She's in Franklin Hall, too, poor little dear. She's all alone now. Raymond was killed in the first bombing of Manila."

Lost and dead husbands—runaways—and he, who had made all manner of promises, only to betray her. If crying would do any good—

But it wouldn't.

Silently Imogene walked up the steps.

twelve

It was midafternoon of the day Imogene and her family arrived that Jimmy drove into Manila. He was on a mission.

He parked the military vehicle just outside the city limits. Due to the shortage of gasoline, motorized transportation was nearly nonexistent on the streets now, and an official car would have created more attention than he wanted. He didn't relish the possibility of having to explain to the commandant should he be seen.

The day had started oppressively hot, made worse by the moisture in the air. The humidity this time of year was another thing to hate about the war.

Seeing Imogene was the first ray of happiness he'd felt since leaving home five months ago. And even that was short lived. The look of hurt and betrayal in her eyes when he pretended not to know her crushed his spirit, even in remembering.

Couldn't she see he had no choice?

He didn't want to be here any more than she did. From the beginning he'd tried to make his father understand. But no. "Your duty is to the emperor," his father had said.

Jimmy's mother had tried to console him. "Don't be troubled, Jimmu. Believe that God has a purpose for you, even in this. Open your heart and mind, and you will find it." When he left, she wept.

His father had curled his lip at her weeping.

Jimmy felt a surge of bitterness, remembering the expression of disdain on his father's face.

He rolled up the car window.

In the past he had taken God for granted, but now He was his solace and hope.

As his mother had urged, he had tried through faith to find the purpose in it all, to find God's purpose for him. Like David in the Bible, he had sought a revelation. So far it had eluded him.

He got out of the car and shoved the keys into his pocket.

Dodging through the bicycle-riding soldiers who streamed up the boulevard like spawning salmon, he maneuvered around the line waiting to eat at the servicemen's cafeteria.

Down the block he paused to look in the window of a converted department store, now a gallery exhibiting propaganda photographs and art.

Not what he'd choose to hang on his wall.

Japanese and Nazi flags hung in the windows of the shops that were still occupied. On the empty buildings were tacked placards from the Imperial General Headquarters with "liberation" directives that promised severe punishment if disobeyed.

Liberation. Whom did they think they were kidding?

He threaded his way through vendors selling a variety of merchandise, no doubt looted from warehouses along the pier. Anything from typewriters and canned goods to baby dresses and fine needlepoint. Sold, he noted, for the price of vegetables.

He decided to turn toward Jones Bridge and find a *carromata* to take him to the university. Since the "liberation," the citizens had used the little carriages drawn by tiny horses, the Philippines' original transportation.

Then he heard the screams.

A manned tank blocked the mouth of the bridge. As he drew closer, he saw a young Filipino boy lashed to one of the treads, his leg twisted beneath it. Blood streamed down his battered face, his gaping mouth the source of the screams.

The tank roared forward, reversed, then forward in an ever-lengthening arc. A few more feet and the boy would be completely crushed.

Without thinking, Jimmy ran toward the tank, his shouts lost in the grind and clamor of its gears.

Slowly the turret swiveled toward him.

He stood, grounded to the spot, his arms outstretched and waving as the tank went from reverse into forward.

And stopped.

The hatch door flew open. The commander's head appeared.

In that instant Jimmy was struck by the sheer lunacy of his act. He was about to defy a superior officer's authority. In the hierarchy of Japanese sins, that ranked just about at the top.

The boy would be crushed to death, and the retribution to Jimmy could only be imagined.

Before the commander had a chance to speak, Jimmy began shouting in Japanese and pointing behind him. "I'm glad I found you! I have come from San Andres Street. Guerrillas are looting the Escolata!"

Immediately the commander's head disappeared again. The door to the hatch slammed shut. Within seconds the engine engaged and the machine roared forward, just as Jimmy cut the hapless youth from the churning tread.

Before Jimmy could blink, the boy was dragged from his arms and swallowed into the surging crowd.

Jimmy wasted no time in commandeering a passing carromata. "Adamson University," he directed the driver.

So he had lied. The lie had saved a life. Two, if he counted his own.

He realized he was still shaking.

The driver turned his head. "You speak English."

Jimmy nodded.

"I see you. A brave thing you do."

"Not really, but thank you." He had acted on instinct. Being brave is knowing the consequences before one acts. He wondered, if he'd had time to think, would he have taken the same risk?

He adjusted in the uncomfortable seat and looked down at the once crisp pleat of his trousers melting in the humid afternoon heat. It would rain soon; he could smell it.

He missed America and everything it stood for. He missed the freedom, the justice, and the bedrock faith in God Almighty. He missed America, but here he was serving her enemy, a country whose values he decried. Either way he felt like a traitor.

At the entrance to Adamson University, Jimmy stepped down from the tiny carriage, instructing the driver to wait. A sentry directed him to the administration offices.

Since the school had been commandeered as a hospital, the records were in disarray, and it took some time to find the address of David Spaneas. Locating Becky's husband, Imogene's brother-in-law, was the very least Jimmy could do for her. He prayed he would find David alive, but he had grave doubts. Surely, if David were alive, he would have found a way to contact his wife. But then, in the turmoil of war, who knew?

"Finally." The pretty Filipina secretary scribbled a number on a sheet of paper. "It's in a suburb of New Manila. Are you familiar with the area?"

"Somewhat. I'm sure my driver will be able to find it. And thank you."

"You speak English very well." The young woman gave

him a coy smile. "Have you been to America?"

"I studied there." In no mood for flirtatious banter, he began inching toward the door. "Thank you very much for your help."

"Anytime," she called after him as he hurried down the hall.

Jimmy had no idea what he would find; so much had been destroyed during the bombing.

To his relief the grand Spanish Colonial home at the address he'd been given was undamaged. It was surrounded by manicured lawns and lush tropical gardens. Tiny orchids hung in profusion from planted baskets that were suspended from the branches of the great trees that lined the sweeping drive.

From all outward appearances at least, it appeared the war had not drastically altered the lifestyle of the Spaneas family.

But as he walked up the front stairs and stepped into the shade of the veranda, his heart sank.

On the door hung a black wreath.

thirteen

After dinner Will Pennington escorted his daughters and Miss Goldie to their dorm and left them for the night.

Their room was empty.

"What a relief. I don't think I have enough energy left to be nice to a bunch of strangers," Imogene said. "Maybe we can fall asleep before they get back—or at least pretend to."

Becky sagged onto her cot and kicked off her sandals. "This may have been the longest day of my life."

"I know." Imogene gave her arm a comforting pat. "Don't be discouraged. First thing tomorrow we'll start asking around about David. Someone is bound to know him. He's from one of the most prominent Greek families in Manila. Would you like me to massage your feet, Sister?" Imogene asked.

"Oh, Imo, would you?"

Imogene sat down on the bed and took Becky's feet into her lap.

Despite her bone-bending fatigue, the montage of thoughts passing through her brain would never allow her to sleep.

An hour later she was still awake when their roommates returned.

"Who are you?" the teenage girls chorused, not bothering to lower their voices.

Imogene raised her finger to her lips and glanced at the adjoining cots.

Neither Becky nor Miss Goldie stirred.

"That's dorm life," Cluny said, her tone only a notch lower.

"You get so you can sleep through anything." She introduced Mavis and Maude Norton and their mother, Betty. Having done her job, she retreated to her cot and picked up her movie magazine.

The twins flopped down on Maude's bed and pulled out a deck of cards. In the next cot their mother curled up with her back against the wall and gathered her knitting.

The girls were short and a bit chubby, with figures not yet formed. They had sly, mischief-making brown eyes and a frizz of flaming hair they'd obviously inherited from their mother, an older and heavier version of the two.

Lights out at eleven. The girls continued to giggle until their mother shushed them quiet.

As Imogene finally drifted off to sleep, she was still reflecting on this new life they were entering, the challenges awaiting them, finding Becky's David, the baby her sister protected within her. And Jimmy, lurking in the shadows of her mind.

The next morning Imogene, Miss Goldie, and Becky dragged themselves out of bed. They fell in line with the rest to use the shower and brush their teeth, then dressed and stumbled into line again for roll call.

Apparently they had no directives from the commandant that morning. Jimmy was nowhere in sight. But he might as well have been, for he was still that much in Imogene's thoughts.

For breakfast, since Becky's condition was "so pathetic," Cluny had agreed to allow Imogene and Becky to use the card table Cluny had set up for herself across from their room in the hall corridor. It was pushed up against the wall and had three folding chairs around it.

Becky eased herself down into a chair and rested her elbow on the table. Listlessly she stirred the mush in her tin pie plate—tin cups and pie plates being their "china."

The sight of the congealing goo squelched even Imogene's appetite. Nevertheless, as a good example, she popped a spoonful into her mouth. "It's not that bad. Please, Becky, try to eat some of it; you need your strength. Later I'll bring you some fruit."

As she took a sip of the tepid, colored water they called coffee, she felt a hand on her arm.

"Imogene Pennington. I looked for you at roll call. I heard you all were here."

Imogene turned and found herself gazing into the animated face of the little lady from the cruise ship that she had once thought of as vaguely pretty and very pale. "Denice Diller. It's good to see you."

Denice was wearing a lovely floral print, with a matching yellow ribbon in her blond bobbed hair, and did not look one bit the grieving widow.

"This is my sister, Becky."

Becky managed a weary smile.

"Nice to meet you, Becky." Denice frowned. "I must say, Dahlin', a young lady with child should not have to eat such unappetizin' food." She looked at Imogene. "You remember how Raymond was about food. It would a' killed him—if he wasn't already dead—to eat what they give us here."

As she spoke, she rummaged around in the large canvas bag she carried and pulled out a mango and a banana and laid them on the table between Imogene and her sister. "Somewhere in here is a knife. Ah!" She brandished it triumphantly. "There now—isn't that better?" Her Southern accent was palpable in its soothing softness.

She perched on the chair between them and began peeling the fruit as she spoke. "I suppose Mrs. Duke told you Raymond was killed."

Imogene nodded. "I'm so sorry."

"It was in the first bombin' attack. We'd hardly gotten off the ship." She rested her hand, holding the knife, and sighed, then began slicing the mango and laying the slices on each of their tin plates in turn.

"How very sad," Becky said.

"It was," Denice said.

"You must miss him terribly."

"For awhile I did. We were used to each other after thirty-two years. Now I can't say I do. I'm afraid my Raymond was not a very nice man." She looked up; her blue eyes were clear. "You remember, Imogene."

Imogene lowered her gaze. How well she remembered.

There was a moment of silence.

"I hope poor Raymond has found peace, wherever he is. I know I have." She looked at Becky and smiled. "You're fortunate, Dahlin'. Raymond and I had no children. He didn't want any. Probably just as well—I doubt he would have made a very good father. But I was sad because of it." Her face brightened. "I'm making up for it now, though. I have a dozen little folks I teach in the camp school."

"That's wonderful, Denice," Imogene said.

"First grade. I love my little dahlin's. Yes, we have our own community goin' within these walls. So far the Japanese have left us pretty much to ourselves, as long as we obey their rules." Denice wrapped the knife in her handkerchief and stood up. "I've got to wash my hands." She paused, as if she were considering her next words.

"Jimmu. . .Jimmy. You saw him, of course."

Imogene nodded.

"He always seemed a gentleman. Not mean like my Raymond. It's strange where circumstances put us. Poor Jimmy.

I doubt he's very happy where he finds himself now. That boy is definitely not at peace. You can see it in his handsome face. Well, dahlin's," she said abruptly, "I must be off. I have to get ready for my babies." She patted Imogene on the shoulder. "We could use a music teacher, Imogene. When you're settled, we'll talk about it. Nice meetin' you, Becky."

"Thank you for the fruit," Becky said.

"There's more where that came from. Raymond was very penurious, you know. Now that he's gone, I'm able to spend for two. Well, bye-bye, y'all." She bounced down the hall with a lightness in her step that Imogene could hardly believe.

If only she, Imogene, could feel anything but her own bitter disappointment.

That afternoon Imogene woke from a nap to find a woman, not much older than her sister, slouched in the doorway of their room, smoking a cigarette. A vision in black in her snug-fitting black dress with a red silk rose blooming in the deep-cut neckline. She had dyed black hair, black-penciled brows, and spiky black lashes around startling, clear blue eyes. Her pouty red lips matched the color of the rose and her stiletto-heeled sandals.

She took a long draw on her cigarette and exhaled slowly, squinting through the smoke. In a husky voice replete with whiskey and tobacco, she asked, "Are you Imogene?"

Imogene nodded.

"I have a message from Jimmy Yamashida."

fourteen

"A message from Jimmy?"

"He wants you to meet him in the music auditorium at three o'clock." The woman took another drag on her cigarette.

So he did know Imogene existed. Her throat constricted.

Maybe she wasn't ready to see *him*.

A cord of bitterness twisted around her heart.

She glanced around the crowded dorm with cots lined up so close that scarcely two feet lay between, and she remembered a room of her own, with a four-poster bed and fresh sheets that smelled of sunshine. She remembered cut-crystal bowls filled with fresh flowers and chocolates.

As the woman exhaled, smoke wafted upward toward her eyes in a diaphanous scrim.

The Japanese had taken it all, destroyed everything lovely and gracious in their lives.

She thought of her last glimpse of Jimmy, arrogant in his military uniform. Jimmy, looking her in the eye without a blink of recognition or compassion.

"You're going, aren't you?" the woman asked.

"Have I a choice?"

The woman shrugged.

"Unless I want to suffer the consequences," Imogene added.

"Jimmy's not that way."

How did this kind of woman know the way Jimmy was? Jimmy was certainly full of surprises.

"He'll be there at three." She turned and began strolling back down the hall in the direction from which she'd come.

"What's your name?" Imogene called after her.

"Gloria," she answered, not looking back.

An hour later Imogene was walking across the campus toward what used to be the music department of the university.

"Hi, Imogene."

She flinched at the sound of the nasal, unctuous voice.

Angier Duke fell into step beside her. "How is everything going? Are you settling in all right?"

"Just fine, Angier. Thank you."

"Call me Angie." His darting eyes focused for a moment on her right cheek. "That's what my friends call me." He giggled nervously. "I do think of you as a friend. I hope you feel the same." He fell silent, waiting for a confirmation.

What could she say? "Of course I think of you as a friend, Angier—Angie."

Internment camps made strange bedfellows. Not necessarily those one would choose under normal circumstances.

"I would have thought you would still be taking your siesta." He quickened his step to keep up with her. "Where are you heading?"

"I thought I'd just walk around, get acquainted with the campus."

"Not much happening during siesta time."

"So I see." How was she going to get rid of him without hurting his feelings?

"If there's anything I can show you, anything you want to know—"

"I'll call on you, Angie. Thank you." There was no way she could meet Jimmy with him on her heels. She speeded up.

Angier kept pace.

"I hope I'm not keeping you from your siesta," she tried hopefully.

"Oh, no. Have you had a chance yet to think about accompanying our chorus?"

"You only asked me yesterday."

"Yes, but—"

They had reached the steps to the music building.

"This is where we practice," Angier said. "In the auditorium."

"Oh. Then they must have a piano."

Imogene walked up the steps and pulled open the door. In the entrance she placed herself to block Angier. "Do you think they'd let me play it?"

"Of course. I'd love to hear you play. I remember on the ship—"

"It's been so long, months since I touched a piano. Would you mind—"

"I'd just sit in the back and not make a peep. You wouldn't even know I was there."

"I know, but you understand." Imogene's voice was definite.

Like a disappointed child, Angier drew his lips into a pout. He sighed. "Very well. Perhaps when you finish, we could meet—"

"Let me check on Becky first—see how she's feeling. She hasn't been all that well."

"I'm so sorry to hear that." His thick black brows braided into a frown. "I hope it's not serious."

"I don't think so. It's just been so hard, her pregnancy and all."

"If there's anything I can do—"

"Just knowing you're nearby is a great help."

Imogene backed through the door and closed it behind her. She leaned against it, heaving a sigh of relief. Poor Angier. He meant well.

But Angier was very little bother considering her other problems.

The music auditorium was small, with an aisle on either side and seating for no more than one hundred or so. In the center of the dimly lit stage at the foot of the room stood a grand piano, its back lid propped open, as if there had just been a concert or one was eminent.

"Imogene." Jimmy's voice floated out of the darkness.

The voice that up until yesterday had echoed in her every dream and fantasy since they'd met, the voice, once so beloved, that had made her heart melt in its warmth, now, for an instant, did so again.

She felt his hand grasp her wrist.

"Immie." His warm breath brushed her ear.

She closed her eyes. She wanted to lean back and feel his strong arms around her. She wanted to feel safe and loved and protected again, as she had when they first met.

Was she out of her mind?

She turned and pushed him away.

In the dimness it was hard to make out the expression on his face.

It was not hard, however, to distinguish the Japanese uniform he wore.

Nor was it hard to identify the feeling of revulsion that swept over her at the sight of it.

He must have sensed her reaction. "Imogene, please, let me explain why—"

"It isn't necessary. It doesn't matter anymore."

"I don't believe that."

"I didn't either, until I saw you yesterday. We're on different sides now, Jimmy. It's simple. There's really no more to be said."

"So why did you come?"

"Frankly, I didn't think I had a choice."

"You know you do," he said quietly.

"So Gloria told me. Whoever she is."

"But you didn't believe her."

"Somehow past experience with your countrymen has not inspired trust. You can imagine why."

"I know how you must feel, but believe me—"

"You have no idea how I feel. I can only pray that someday, God willing, you will find out." She turned away from him and began to move toward the door.

"Where are you going?"

She had to get out of there. She felt as if she were smothering. "I think we're finished."

"Actually not. I think you'd better sit down, Imogene."

"I don't—"

"Sit down," he commanded.

She hesitated, but the firmness in his voice frightened her a little. She slid into the aisle seat in the last row.

Shoving his hands into his trouser pockets, he looked down at her, then allowed his gaze to drift to the lighted stage. His expression was morose.

The only sound in the empty auditorium was the jangle of the keys he played with in his pocket.

Abruptly he stopped. "I was able to find out what happened to David."

"You were?" She started to rise, but he put his hand on her shoulder and held her in her seat.

"Oh, no," she moaned.

"He's dead."

"Oh, no. Oh, dear God, no." Imogene felt as if her heart had been sucked out of her, and a hopelessness and despair deeper than anger, deeper than tears, filled the void it left. "Poor Becky. Poor Becky."

Jimmy reached out, but she held up her hand to ward him off. "When did it happen? How?"

"Right after the occupation. He was caught at the university, harboring guerrillas."

"And?"

"The Japanese. He was executed."

Imogene covered her face with her hands and felt the tears spill through her fingers. She sobbed, her pain more insistent than her will to control it. She'd always known David's death was a possibility, but now, with Jimmy's words, it had become a reality.

She felt his hand on her shoulder and shrugged it away. But as her sobs slowly subsided, she accepted the handkerchief he offered.

She wiped her eyes. "With David dead, what about the baby? Who will take care of Becky and the baby? We have nothing left. No money, nothing. The Japanese have left us nothing."

"Imogene, I'm so sorry."

"I'm sure you are." She couldn't look at him. "I know this has been difficult for you. Thank you for finding out."

"You don't need to thank me."

"I do." She had to thank him because she had one more favor to ask now. She hated to beg, to put herself in a position of owing him anything. But her need was greater than her pride.

Lifting her eyes, in the faint light, she saw his haggard face and the downward turn of his mouth.

"When Becky's time comes, she's going to need help. If the Spaneases, David's family, are able, is there any way we can get her out of this place and released to them?"

"You saw how our commandant is about Americans—"

"Forget I asked," Imogene interrupted. "It's not your problem anyway."

"You know I'll do what I can."

fifteen

Jimmy cautioned Imogene to keep their meeting to herself and had her leave the music building first so as not to arouse suspicion.

As she stumbled down the front steps, lost in her own sad thoughts, Angier pounced.

"You don't look at all well, Imogene, not at all well." His pale, red-rimmed eyes narrowed. "Did something happen in there to disturb you?"

Imogene didn't answer but accelerated her pace in an effort to discourage him.

Angier hurried to keep up. "I didn't hear the piano." When she didn't answer, he continued. "I admit, I stood in the foyer hoping for a little concert. I know you didn't want me to. I just supposed if you didn't know it wouldn't matter."

Suddenly he grabbed her arm. His grip was amazingly strong.

"You weren't completely honest with me, Imogene. You were meeting someone in there. I heard voices." He pursed his lips. "Was it Jimmy Yamashida?"

Imogene yanked her hand away. She wanted to slap his face. She wanted to scream at him, *Leave me alone! Can't you see that something terrible and sad has happened?* But she didn't. "He brought bad news" was all she said and ran toward the dorm.

Angier didn't matter. What difference did it make if he knew about Jimmy? Only one thing mattered now: How was she going to break the tragic news to Becky? And where? Where in this tangled mass of humanity could she find a private place for the family to be alone?

Quietly she approached Denice Diller. Maybe not the best solution, but a private shanty was better than their dorm, with Cluny propped on her cot in the corner reading old movie magazines and the twins arguing with their mother.

"Certainly, Dahlin', you're welcome to use my place for that sad task. Most folks will be at the barbershop quartet competition in the plaza, so it should be relatively private for y'all."

Denice had left a bowl of fresh fruit in the middle of the little table around which they now gathered. She had made some cookies on her little ceramic stove and a pitcher of lemonade, without ice of course.

Almost immediately Becky sensed something was wrong. "Funny that Denice would invite us here, go to all this trouble, and then leave." She looked around the table. "What is it? What's wrong?"

Imogene cleared her throat. "Becky—"

Becky's troubled eyes widened with the dawning realization of what she was about to hear. "You found out something about David."

Her father reached across the table and covered her hand with his.

"Is he hurt?" She searched their faces. "Oh, no, he's not dead. Don't tell me he's dead. No!" She turned her head from side to side. "No, I won't believe it. No, oh, please, no!" she wailed. Pulling her hand from her father's, she covered her mouth with her clenched fists. Her brown eyes were huge with anguish. "Oh, dear God, no!"

It was heartbreaking. Imogene sat next to her, desperately

wanting to say something of comfort, but she couldn't find the words. She felt so helpless.

The lines of her father's face etched deeper with sorrow as Miss Goldie drew the grief-stricken girl into her arms. Swept up in the torrent of Becky's tears, all they could do was wait. Slowly her sobs began to subside until finally, drained of strength and will, her head sank against Miss Goldie's shoulder.

Miss Goldie held her close, stroking her long, dark hair and murmuring quiet words of comfort. Despite her gentle nature and soft voice, Miss Goldie had a core of strength that supported them all. Now more than ever.

"David is in safe hands, Rebecca," she said. "Be comforted by God's promise. Remember—Jesus is the 'resurrection and the life: he that believeth in me, though he were dead, yet shall he live: and whosoever liveth and believeth in me, shall never die.'"

That was all very well and good for David, Imogene thought, but what about Becky? Where was the comfort in it for her?

Miss Goldie took a clean hankie from her pocket and wiped Becky's tear-sodden cheek.

All of her life Imogene had accepted without question God, maker of heaven and earth, source of all that was beautiful and good. Where was that God now? She looked up and found her father's troubled gaze on her. Did he suspect her doubts?

"I love him so much. What am I going to do without him? I don't want to live without him," Becky moaned.

Miss Goldie held Becky's face in her hands and looked into her eyes. "Oh, my darling girl, you mustn't say that. You mustn't even think it. You have that dear baby inside you.

David's and your baby—who needs your love and cherishing even more now. You have so much to live for." She drew Becky's head back against her shoulder. "Jesus promised, 'Blessed are they that mourn: for they shall be comforted.' It may not seem so now, but in time you will find comfort. Believe me—you will."

Promises, promises, Imogene thought bitterly. She looked over at her sister.

As Miss Goldie soothed and stroked Becky, Becky's eyes closed; and although from time to time her body trembled with little sobbing sighs, to Imogene's surprise, her face grew calm.

"Perhaps we should return to the dorm. Sleep would be good for us all." Miss Goldie looked over at Becky's father.

"I think—" He cleared his throat. Tears glistened in his eyes. A quiet man, not one to flaunt his emotions, but his faith in God and his love for his family had always been deeply felt.

"Before we separate, could we bow our heads for a moment of prayer?" As he began, his voice, usually so strong and confident, trembled slightly. "Most merciful Father, who has taken unto Yourself the soul of Your servant David, grant to us, who are still on our pilgrimage, the purpose and strength to carry on, so we may fulfill the work You have intended us to do. Help us to forgive those who have persecuted us, as Jesus forgave those who persecuted Him. May we be instruments of Your peace in a world that is so desperately in need of it. In Jesus' precious name, we pray. Amen."

Imogene clasped her sister's slender hand and that of her dear father, and for that moment at least her troubled heart was calmed.

sixteen

Jimmy sat at his desk trying to ignore the commandant's abrasive bellowing at a hapless sergeant in the adjoining office as he thought about Imogene and the untenable task she had asked of him.

He knew how dangerous it would be for them both if the commandant found out he had met with her last week. Even more dangerous if he found out they'd had a prior relationship. At best, Jimmy would be punished; at worst, transferred. Either way he would no longer be able to protect her.

Wearily he dropped his head onto his crossed arms on the desk. "Dear God," he murmured, "please give me an idea of what I can do to help them." They had suffered so much. He sat up and absently began to sort the sheets of requisitions on his desk, putting them in appropriate piles for the commandant's signature.

He paused, stared at the paper in his hand, put it down, and stared at it again. Then he slipped a page into his typewriter and typed in his request, leaving blank the line at the bottom. He stuck it in the middle of the pile, lost among the other sheets to be signed.

❧

It was midafternoon, and the dorm was empty except for Imogene and Becky. Imogene sat on her cot, her back propped against the wall, a book open in her lap. It might as well have been closed for all the reading she had done.

It had been over a week since her conversation with Jimmy.

If he was making any progress toward getting Becky out of the camp, he gave no sign. From the beginning she had wondered if his "I'll try" had been merely a way of placating her. An idle promise. Time would tell. She sighed, glad she'd had the wisdom not to mention the possibility of escape to Becky.

She looked over at her sister, napping on the cot next to her. The support of David's family since they'd learned of Becky's internment had helped. As Greeks, they had not been imprisoned as the Americans were, and they visited outside the gate regularly, bringing her nourishing food and loving encouragement.

But clearly Becky's strength came from her belief in a loving and protective God. A conclusion, in the face of such devastating grief, that Imogene could not understand.

One of the twins tiptoed into the room, pulled a checkerboard from the stash of games under her bed, and tiptoed out again.

Their roommates had responded to the tragedy with an unexpected kindness. Even the twins had been more considerate than Imogene thought possible for energetic thirteen year olds. She wondered how long it would last.

Miss Goldie appeared in the door holding a package. "It's for you," she whispered, handing it to Imogene. "Amazing how quickly the Red Cross managed to track you down."

"Seems like an eternity to me." This was the first package any of them had received.

"You don't have to whisper. I'm awake." Becky sat up and dropped her feet to the floor. She rubbed her protruding belly.

If Jimmy didn't come up with something soon, time would not only tell, but it would also run out.

"Who is it from?" Becky asked, revealing her own excitement.

"My college roommate, Daisy," Imogene said, studying

the return address. "It was mailed in March. Went first to Negros." She tore open the box.

On top was Daisy's letter.

"Read it aloud," Becky said. "I'm dying to hear what's happening in America."

"I suspect anything worth hearing about will be censored," Imogene said. She glanced down the page. "What a surprise! Nothing's blacked out." She cleared her throat and began.

Dear Imo,

How life has changed here at Oxy. At first the war seemed so far away, and I'm afraid I saw it as quite glamorous. The boys looking so handsome, dashing about importantly in their new uniforms.

"That sounds like Daisy," Imogene murmured. "Always alert to what's important."

I must say, though, that it didn't take long for my attitude to change. We're not just playing at war; this is the real thing. Aside from the silly little inconveniences like running out of colas in the beverage machine and that yucky oleo margarine instead of butter, we've painted all the windows in the dorms black and collected scrap metal. Some of the boys have become fire wardens and learned about incendiary bombs. I even picked up a shovel and filled sandbags.

Imogene looked up. "From the girl who can't stand to perspire."

As for me personally, I've become quite proficient at

first aid, and I'm on the "Dance for Defense"
Committee—

"That figures." Imogene laughed.

We moved the Wednesday night mixer to the girls' gym
and charge a ten-cent defense stamp admission fee.
You'd be amazed at how many we collect. I'm also
learning to knit so I can knit sweaters for the Red Cross.
  So you can see, I'm not the frivolous scatterbrain you
once thought I was. I'm doing my bit for the war effort,
but I'm missing you dreadfully.

"I miss you, too, dear Daisy." Imogene folded the letter.
They were worlds apart now, in distance and in experience,
but certainly not in heart.

"I can't wait to see what she sent you," Becky said.

"Knowing Daisy, I'm sure it will all be very practical."
Imogene grinned. She rummaged around in the box and drew
out a smart green pouch. "Ah, a makeup kit. Just what I've
needed." She unzipped the kit and laid it flat open in front of
her on the cot. "And look—it has special pockets for the
important beauty necessities."

"Like an eyelash curler," Becky cried, picking it up and
demonstrating how it worked. She handed it to Miss Goldie,
who giggled like a schoolgirl and followed suit.

"And nail polish," Imogene said. "My favorite color. And
two bottles."

"One for your fingers and one for your toes," Becky said.

Imogene dug deeper into the box and pulled out—"Ta
da!"—a double box of See's candy. She held it just out of her
sister's reach.

"Oh, Imo, *really.*" With mock disgust, Becky grabbed the box, ripped it open, and popped a truffle in her mouth before Imogene could snatch it back.

"Don't eat it all at once. We've got to make it last."

"Remember what Cluny said about wearing our valuables," Becky reminded her, shoving another bonbon into her mouth. "What better way."

Again Imogene rummaged in the box and pulled out—

"A snood." Becky cackled.

Imogene tied the band around her head and tucked her bob of dark hair into the woven net pouch. She assumed a model's pose. "Do I look glamorous?"

"Indeed you do. Let's see how Rebecca looks in it," Miss Goldie suggested.

Looking in a hand mirror that had accompanied the makeup kit, Becky giggled as Miss Goldie tucked her long, dark hair into the snood.

"Hey, Imogene." Gloria stood in the doorway. Smoke from the cigarette dangling in the corner of her mouth snaked around her head. She wore a short green sheath, so snug that if it had been any tighter, it would have looked as if it were tattooed on her.

Crooking her index finger for Imogene to follow, she waited in the hall, one hand resting on her cocked hip. The ash from her cigarette dropped toward the floor, intercepted by her generous bosom. Her voice was low and covert. "Jimmy wants you to meet him in the music room at four."

seventeen

Jimmy looked out his office window. From where he stood, he could see the entrance to the music building. He glanced at his watch. Five minutes to four. Imogene should be arriving any minute.

He dreaded this meeting almost as much as he had their first. In fact, it had taken him several days to work up the courage to give her the bad news.

He thought back on the day the commandant had, in his own inimitable way, denied the request. Jimmy still smarted from the confrontation.

&

"What is this?" the commandant had roared, throwing the sheet of paper down on his desk.

Jimmy picked it up. "It looks like a request from one of the internees, Sir."

"I suspect you, Lieutenant—"

Jimmy froze.

"I suspect you of being too easy on these people." He squinted up at Jimmy. "You college boys are all alike. Soft." His tone was surly and belittling. He snatched the paper from Jimmy's hand, tore it into quarters, and dropped the pieces into the wastebasket beside his desk. "No more, or I will be forced to discipline you." He picked up his pen. "Dismissed."

"Very good, Sir."

&

Jimmy looked nervously at his watch again. Only two minutes had passed. He wanted to be sure she was there before he went in. He dared take no chances of raising suspicion. There had been too many small acts that had caught the commandant's attention. He didn't want the man to add them up and see a pattern.

Ah, there she was.

Who was that with her? It was hard to tell, squinting into the sun. Wait—it was Angier Duke.

He watched as the two crossed the quad. Angier was animated and kept touching her arm. At the foot of the steps to the music building, he grabbed her hand.

At least she didn't allow him to hold it for long.

Jimmy felt an uncomfortable surge of jealousy. Surely Imogene wasn't interested in Angier Duke?

Now the fellow was following her up the steps.

Well, finally. After a brief conversation, Imogene disappeared through the double doors alone.

For several minutes Angier hung around, looking nervously up at the entrance as if he were about to go after her.

Impatiently, Jimmy crossed his arms. He dared not make his move until he was sure nobody would interrupt them.

At last, with a dispirited shrug, Angier hunched his narrow shoulders and walked back across the quad in the direction from which he'd come.

Jimmy raced out of his office and down the hall. As he reached the front entrance, he saw the commandant hurrying down the steps ahead of him. Jimmy hesitated and moved back into the shadows. To his dismay, the man crossed the lawn and headed, of all places, toward the music building. He strode up the steps two at a time and pushed open the door.

The commandant's office, adjacent to Jimmy's, had a window that offered the same view of the quad. Obviously he, too, had seen Imogene enter the music building.

Jimmy was frantic. There was no doubt about the man's

intentions. More than once he had been outraged at hearing tales from other soldiers who had witnessed behavior that bore out their commandant's reputation with women.

The thought of his precious Imogene being subjected to the savage attention of this monster horrified him. Throwing caution aside, he strode out of his office. Then stopped. Too much was at stake.

❧

Imogene searched the little theater and, seeing that Jimmy had not yet arrived, moved down the aisle and ascended the four steps to the stage. The piano drew her like a magnet.

It had been so long since she'd played.

She adjusted the stool, sat down, and pushed back the fall board. Then, lifting her hands, she ran her fingers lightly over the keys, at first in random chords and then in melody. Without intention, she was playing the Brahms folk song she'd played the night she and Jimmy had met.

She heard the auditorium door open and stopped. "Do you remember when—"

Only it wasn't Jimmy. Too late, she realized.

The commandant stood at the back of the auditorium, the solid bulk of his silhouette unmistakable.

What had she just said? Had she given anything away?

Her throat constricted.

She couldn't remember.

By this time the commandant was marching down the aisle toward her.

What had happened to Jimmy?

She stood and bowed, not daring to meet the man's eyes.

"Pray," the commandant commanded, striding up the steps.

"Pray?"

He nodded.

Did he plan to kill her?

Imogene's blood turned to ice. Jimmy had said the man was crazy.

She saw the holstered gun in his belt. Was he going to shoot her in the head just because she'd requested a release for her pregnant sister? Could he be that crazy? And where was Jimmy? Had he meted out the same punishment to the messenger as he was about to mete out to her?

She dared not disobey his orders. If he said pray, that's what she'd do. And mean every word.

Oh, dear God, help me.

She lifted her clasped hands and bent her head. In a wavery voice, she began to repeat the Lord's Prayer. "Our Father who art in heaven, hallowed be Thy—"

"No, no!" the commandant shouted impatiently. "I say pray." He pointed at the piano. "Pray more."

Imogene almost fainted. He meant *play.* "You want me to play the piano." She pointed to the instrument. "Right?"

"Light!" He nodded vigorously.

This might not turn out to be her best performance, but she would always remember it as the performance of her life.

Relief barely conveyed what she felt. She dropped back onto the stool and lifted her hands—

The commandant walked to the side of the piano where he could look down at her while she played. "My brother pray horn in Yokohama Symphony," he said.

"Chopin," she said. "Nocturne in C sharp minor."

As she played, he nodded his head in time with the music. "Beautifah," he murmured and moved to stand behind her. He put his hands on her shoulders. "Beautifah music. Beautifah rady."

He moved his hand down her arm.

eighteen

Frantic, Jimmy returned to his office. He paced back and forth in front of the window, praying, one eye on the entry to the music building, the other on his watch. It had been fifteen minutes, and neither Imogene nor the commandant had come out.

His imagination ran rampant picturing in lurid detail the awful possibilities of what could be happening behind the auditorium doors.

Hang the consequences. He had to do something. Now!

As he ran across the lawn and up the steps, he prayed that God would protect her. Racing across the lobby, he thrust open the auditorium door.

He saw the commandant hovering over her, his hands moving down her arms.

He saw Imogene's face masked in fear as she struggled to pull away.

"Sir!" Jimmy called out.

The commandant's and Imogene's heads turned simultaneously. But even as she jumped to her feet, the commandant did not release her. His voice was furious. "What are you doing here?" he demanded in Japanese.

Jimmy ran down the aisle, halting at the foot of the steps leading up to the stage. "Sir." He saluted. "Uh—you have an important call from headquarters. I am sorry to interrupt you, Sir, but it demands your immediate attention."

A growl of indignation rose from the commandant's throat as he reluctantly thrust Imogene aside and stormed down the steps. "This had better be important," he said, as if Jimmy would be to blame if it weren't.

Little did he know.

Jimmy would cross that bridge when he came to it.

He waited until the commandant had marched out the door; then he turned to Imogene.

Her face was still in shock. "Jimmy—"

He shook his head and held his finger to his lips. Very quietly and with haste, he said, "I wasn't able to get your sister released. I'm sorry." He turned and started to move toward the door, then paused again. "And I'm sorry I got you into this. It won't happen again."

He hurried after the commandant, contemplating how he would explain the supposed mix-up in the telephone call from headquarters, and was not at all pleased to encounter Angier Duke skulking around at the bottom of the steps.

They stared at each other.

Angier lifted his nose and would have glared down it had Jimmy not been a head taller than he. But what the slight man lacked in stature, he made up for in disdain, as he pushed past Jimmy and scurried up the steps.

❧

Imogene rarely saw Jimmy in the weeks that followed— except at roll call. And then he was uncharacteristically brusque. From time to time he shot her a covert glance when for an instant their gazes connected. After one such exchange she looked up to find Angier Duke assessing her with a look of disapproval.

Ever since that last meeting, when Jimmy had stormed into the auditorium as her protector, Angier had hardly given her a moment's peace. She'd tried to be sensitive to his feelings. Unfortunately he read her kindness as attraction, which could not have been further from the truth. If anything, as time went on, she had discovered more disagreeable aspects of his character and found his presence increasingly distasteful.

It seemed that Denice Diller had also picked up on the exchanges between Imogene and Jimmy and brought it up one evening as they all sat around the table after dinner.

She had invited the family, including Miss Goldie, to share her shanty at mealtimes. Unfortunately the Dukes were just next door, and too often they included themselves in the conversations.

"I think Jimmu Yamashida still holds a soft spot for you, Imogene," Denice said. "I saw the way he looked at you this morning at roll call. It isn't the first time I've noticed it."

Miss Goldie glanced across the table at Imogene's father with an I-told-you-so expression.

"How come I missed it, Imo?" Becky chided.

"There's nothing to miss." Imogene tossed Denice an agitated glance. "The only contact I have with Jimmy is when he brings bad news."

"You can't blame him for that," Becky said.

"I can," Imogene replied, wishing the whole conversation would go away.

"Don't be too hard on him, Imogene," Denice said. "I see him as a victim, too. It's clear he's not at all happy to be here. And he does his best to intercede with the commandant on our behalf."

"His best being none too good," Imogene said. They didn't know the half of it.

"Denice is right. Don't be so hard on the boy," her father said.

"At least he tries," Miss Goldie said.

"Which is more than I can say for most of them," he added.

"Could it be that he's trying to salve his conscience?" *And well he should,* Imogene thought. "He's still a Japanese soldier, regardless of what we think. As such, the less I have to do with him, the better." Did she really mean that?

"It relieves me to hear you say that, my dear." Angier offered through the open window.

She could have kicked herself.

The shanties were close enough to reach out and hold hands, if one were so inclined.

"Imogene's right," Mrs. Duke said across the narrow space, as she sat next to Angier. "They are all cut from the same cloth."

Not exactly what Imogene had meant, but she didn't want to get into it now.

Mrs. Duke went on. "The veneer may be more polished on some, but the soul is still the same. They're all rotten to the core."

"Aren't they showing a movie in the plaza tonight?" Miss Goldie leaped in before Imogene could respond.

Imogene was in no position to defend Jimmy, nor did she want to, but "rotten to the core"? The Dukes were getting more and more on her nerves.

She stood up and began to clear the plates. "I think they're having a quiz tournament before the movie. You don't want to miss that, Angie. You'd have a real good chance of winning."

"Why, thank you, Imogene."

You're such a know-it-all.

"You folks go on," her father said, rising. "Imogene and I will clean up and meet you over there."

"Uh-oh, a daddy-daughter talk. Are you sure you can handle this alone, Imo?" Becky grinned.

"Have I a choice?"

"I guess not." Becky stood up, put her hands in the small of her back, and stretched.

"You're a little flushed, Denice dear. Are you feeling up to par?" Miss Goldie asked as she and Denice were leaving the shack.

"Just a bit tired. But they're showing a Deanna Durbin movie tonight, and I'd hate to miss it."

Imogene's father scraped the plates and put them into the pot of heated soapy water. "What's going on between you and this young soldier, Imogene?"

"Nothing."

"Don't tell me 'nothing.' I have eyes."

"Nothing personal." She began washing the dishes.

Her father's "Uh-huh" sounded skeptical. He picked up the dish towel.

Imogene rested her soapy hands on the edge of the pot and looked at her father. "All right. I'll tell you, if you promise not to mention it to Becky."

"What does Becky have to do with it?"

Imogene related her efforts through Jimmy to get Becky released. "I didn't mention it because I didn't want you all to get your hopes up, in case it didn't happen." She finished washing the last plate and laid it in the rinse pan. "Which, as it turns out, was wise since it didn't. That's about it. As I said, nothing personal. You don't have to worry, Daddy. I don't want anything to do with him."

"I assume he feels the same way."

"He said as much." Imogene remembered Jimmy's last words as he left the auditorium: *It won't happen again.*

Her father shook his head. "It's a pity how circumstances beyond our control can determine the course we take. Goldie seemed to think well of him."

So it was "Goldie" now, not "Miss" Goldie. Imogene smiled to herself.

"Goldie said he has more than charm—he has character," her father said.

"And he can sing? Did Miss Goldie tell you that? And that he's smart and he played college football? Why, he was almost as American as apple pie. He fooled us all." Imogene looked away. "Can you imagine me in love with a—with a Japanese soldier?"

"He wasn't a soldier when you met him."

"He may not have been wearing a uniform, but he was the same person," she said sharply.

"And a pretty nice one, according to Goldie."

"You sound as if you're defending him."

"I'm not—"

Imogene interrupted. "How can you defend any Japanese after what they've done to you—to us? Look at us." She spread her arms. "Look where we are. They've abused us, murdered those we love, stolen everything we own, thrown us into prison—" She took a gulp of air. "And we've gotten off easy. We're still alive—if you call this living."

Her father opened his mouth to speak, but she cut him off. "And don't give me that old saw about 'hate the sin but love the sinner.' It won't fly, Daddy. They're all evil, even Jimmy—"

She had to believe that. If she didn't, every time she looked at him, her heart would break again. "He had a choice."

"Did he?"

"He knew what was going on in China. He wasn't proud of it—or so he said. He could have stayed in the United States. But, no, he chose to trot back to his rich daddy in Japan like the obedient little son of the sun that he is." Imogene closed her eyes and rubbed her temples. She'd had this conversation with herself more times than she could count, and still it hurt.

"I'm not sure he did have a choice, Imogene. That young

man is as much a product of his culture and upbringing as you are of yours. Unquestioning obedience to authority has been ingrained in him since the day he was born." Her father gave her a sardonic smile. "Unlike some cheeky American lasses I can think of."

Imogene crossed her arms. "You *are* defending him."

"I'm not defending him. I don't even know him." Her father put both hands on the table and leaned forward. "And I'm not suggesting that you have anything to do with him. Clearly that would be dangerous. Still I wish him no ill. But he's not my concern. You are. I don't like what I see happening to you, your lack of compassion, the bitterness, the pride."

Imogene's tone turned harsh. "It's the only thing we have left. What else have we if not our pride?"

"Our faith. We still have our faith," her father said quietly.

"In what? You talk about faith. How can I have faith in a God who allows such terrible things to happen?"

"We can't have it both ways, Imogene. God has given us the gift of free choice. With free choice come consequences and responsibilities."

"Oh, I get it. We take the consequences for the irresponsibilities of the Japanese."

"Sadly that sometimes happens. But you can't blame God for that. God's plan is good and perfect. You cannot blame Him for its corruption by men." He touched her shoulder. "But even then, from this—this caldron of despair, I've seen acts of courage and compassion I never thought possible, and from folks I never thought had it in them. How else would I have seen it? How else could they have discovered such goodness in themselves? That's part of God's plan, too." Behind his spectacles, her father's gray eyes mirrored his conviction.

She knew his profound disappointment. She wished she

could accept the God he believed in, as she had when she was a child. But she wasn't a child anymore. She just couldn't.

Her father seemed to sense her withdrawal. He sat down.

Imogene came around the table and embraced him. She leaned down and rubbed her cheek against his as she had as a little girl. "You have enough faith for us both, Daddy."

"Not so, Imogene. But I haven't given up. As Paul said to the Corinthians: 'Our hope of you is stedfast, knowing, that as ye are partakers of the sufferings, so shall ye be also of the consolation.' "

nineteen

Imogene was in no mood for a movie. Of course she'd also be missing the Japanese travelogue and propaganda film that always preceded the show. A loss she did not regret.

She lay back on her cot in the empty dorm, locked her hands behind her head, and closed her eyes. Not to sleep but to ponder what her father had said. Why was she plagued with so many doubts when she'd been brought up by a man with such profound faith? Why did she always need concrete proof for everything, have to touch, see, smell everything, to believe it existed?

Some things couldn't be seen or felt, and yet they were just as real. Those qualities Daddy had talked about, like love and generosity, kindness. She believed in those.

And if she did, didn't the rest of what he'd said make sense? How else would they have known that Pedro, the foreman of their plantation, would be willing to sacrifice his life for theirs; or how the doctors here in the camp kept trying even without the supplies and equipment they needed; or about folks like Denice Diller, who'd found her purpose—God's purpose—in working with the children? And Miss Goldie and Daddy, who, despite all they had suffered and lost, harbored no hate for the sinner, only the sin. And her sister, Becky. Especially Becky.

Grudgingly, she had to admit that through this experience, she might even have discovered a different Imogene. Perhaps a little less self-centered, with a bit more courage than she'd expected, and certainly more resourceful than the girl who had sailed into the harbor at Dumaguete.

Was that less than a year ago? It seemed a lifetime.

She thought of the island where she'd grown up and her plantation home. She remembered those last weeks surrounded by the beauty of the jungle. If she needed the proof of touch, sight, and smell, it was certainly there. What was it Miss Goldie had said? "It's like waking in a cathedral."

Maybe she was trying too hard to explain God. Maybe God was beyond what words could describe.

"Imo, Imo, wake up."

"I'm awake." Imogene opened her eyes to see her sister and Miss Goldie. "What's the matter?"

Miss Goldie sat down on the cot next to her. "Denice Diller got sick in the middle of the movie. Fortunately, Gloria—"

"—who is a nurse, it seems," Becky inserted.

"—was there to help her back to the dorm."

"Gloria says it looks as if she has a case of the measles." Becky clasped her hands over her stomach. "If that's what it is, I'm really worried, Imo. If I were to catch them, it could seriously harm the baby."

Imogene sat up. "Three children were missing from my music class today. Did you have any, Miss Goldie?" The two of them had started teaching at the camp school soon after they arrived.

"Come to think of it—Sofia Rose wasn't there, nor was little Jack Bane."

"Oh, Miss Goldie, I hope we're not seeing the start of an epidemic," Imogene said.

Becky's eyes widened with concern.

"Now, girls," Miss Goldie said. "We don't know for sure that's what it is. Let's not think the worst just yet."

Footsteps down the hall and shrill laughter signaled the return of their roommates.

With their usual teenage exuberance, Mavis and Maude raced into the room in midconversation and bounded onto Maude's bed.

"Spare me that Deanna Durbin opera stuff," Mavis said.

"Me, too. Give me 'Chattanooga Choo Choo' any day," her sister replied.

"Stop bouncing on the cot, girls—you'll break the legs," said their mother, Betty.

Cluny strolled in a minute later and looked over at Imogene and Becky. "What are you two looking so glum about?"

"We think Denice Diller might have the measles," Becky said.

"So?" Cluny plopped down on her cot and picked up the magazine lying open beside her.

"So it can be very dangerous for the baby if a pregnant woman gets the measles," Imogene said, annoyed by Cluny's nonchalance.

"Oh, yeah?" Cluny looked up from her magazine. "I didn't know that. I'm sorry." Her apology sounded genuine enough.

At that moment Gloria stuck her head in the room. "Bad news, ladies. Denice has a rash. I'm afraid it is the measles. Turns out hers isn't the only case that's been reported." Gloria pointed her lighted cigarette at Becky. "You better be real careful, Lady. Well, gotta get back to my patient."

"Even if it isn't an epidemic, we've spent so much time with Denice, I'm sure I've been exposed," Becky said.

"That doesn't mean you're going to get them." What Imogene didn't tell her sister was that she was hatching another plan. First thing in the morning, she would give Jimmy one more try.

❧

Jimmy happened to glance out his office window as Imogene came marching across the quad.

What was she doing?

He jumped up from his desk.

Was she crazy? What if the commandant happened to be looking out his window as Jimmy was?

Rushing out into the hall, he noticed, to his relief, that the commandant's door was closed. He hurried out the front entrance as Imogene came barreling up the steps, head down, and bumped into him.

"Jimmy!"

"Are you crazy? What are you doing here, Imogene?" His voice was low and angry.

"Oh, Jimmy, something terrible has happened, and you're the only one I can turn to. Becky—"

As she spoke, he took her by the arm and half-dragged, half-carried her around to the back of the building.

"What are you doing? Get your hands off me!"

He glared down at her. "You're such a naive, impossible woman, Imogene. Do you know how dangerous it is for you to be here?"

She tried to pull away, but he wouldn't let go.

"Do you?" They were nose to nose.

He could smell the sweetness of her, see the fine lines around the pupil of her eyes. Each curling lash was in his sights. It was hard to stay angry when he stood that close.

Imogene yanked free. She rubbed her arm as she spoke. "Please hear me out."

He could see this was not easy on her pride. "Very well. But be quick about it."

"There may be a measles epidemic. Some of the children

have them, and last night Denice Diller came down with them."

"I'm sorry to hear that, but what do you expect me to do about it?" Jimmy asked impatiently. "I'm not a doctor." He just wanted Imogene out of there.

"I'm not finished. As you can probably tell, my sister is *quite* pregnant. If she were to get the measles, it could be very dangerous for her baby."

"Imogene—"

"If you don't believe me, ask your pal, Nurse Gloria."

"Will you please keep your voice down?" Jimmy muttered. "And I don't need to talk to Gloria. I believe you."

"You've got to get Becky out of here, Jimmy."

He could hear the desperation in her voice and see it in the reckless beauty of her violet eyes.

"I can't, Imogene. Don't you understand? I tried, and I can't."

"Then I'll go to the commandant myself."

Before she could make a move, Jimmy grabbed her arm again.

Imogene flinched, then struggled.

This time he wasn't about to let her go. "You can't do that."

"I can, and I will. You leave me no other choice."

"Imogene, I cannot tell you how dangerous that would be for you. Once you're involved with this man, there's no way to get away from him. You will endanger not only yourself but your entire family. He is ruthless. Do you understand me?"

She nodded.

She may have understood, but did she believe him? He couldn't hold on to her like this forever. He took a deep breath. "Look. Give me a little bit of time. A day or two. Maybe I can come up with something."

"You have to."

"I know."

She let out a great breath of air, as if she'd been holding strong for as long as she could, and now all the strength poured out of her with that one long breath. She sagged against him.

He wrapped his arms around her, felt her softness—but for no more than a heartbeat.

He pushed her away. "I'll get word to you through Gloria. Now go! And avoid the quad. The commandant's office overlooks it, too. If he'd seen you, he might have been out here, not me."

He didn't wait for her response. He couldn't bear to be near her another minute, to see the anguish in her eyes or smell her fragrance or be near enough to touch her and not do so.

There was just so much a person could take.

He turned and bounded up the steps without looking back.

twenty

Jimmy's previous willingness to help Imogene had been hapless, at best. So she wasn't much surprised when after two days she had heard nothing. Oh, she'd seen him at roll call, but he didn't so much as glance in her direction.

She had hoped for more. After her conversation with her father, she had been willing—had desperately *wanted*—to give him the benefit of the doubt. But once again she had dared to hope and found him wanting.

If he didn't contact her by tonight, she would go to the commandant herself, take her chances. Her mind was made up.

Her father napped in a hammock they had strung between the two main poles of the shack, and Becky sat with her swollen feet raised while Imogene and Miss Goldie cleaned up after the evening meal.

Miss Goldie looked over at the older man with concern. "Your father's hardly eaten anything all day. Look how flushed he is."

"I'd noticed that, too," Becky said. "I just thought he'd gotten more sun than usual, working in the vegetable garden."

"He didn't feel up to it today. That's what worries me. He's so dedicated to that garden. I tried to get him to go to the infirmary, but you know men." She shook her head. "He says he's just getting a cold. I'm concerned it's the measles."

"Didn't you tell him there's an epidemic?" Imogene asked.

"He says only children get the measles."

"Denice is no child."

"I pointed that out."

"If you can't convince him, Miss Goldie, no one can."

Miss Goldie blushed.

Over her head Imogene's eyes met Becky's. There was more to the relationship than either their father or Miss Goldie was willing to let on.

The prospect that her father might have come down with the measles made Imogene even more determined to exhaust every possibility to get Becky out of the festering epidemic.

Even though the Spaneases, David's family, contributed what they could, poor nutrition and fatigue were beginning to tell on Becky. Imogene knew her sister lacked the physical resources to withstand a major illness without endangering her own life and that of her baby.

It had been no idle threat when she'd told Jimmy she would go to the commandant. She knew the risk. But what was her risk compared to the life of Becky and her unborn child?

With each passing hour, her hope of hearing from Jimmy diminished until by curfew she had none left.

Her self-imposed deadline had passed.

Imogene did not sleep well that night.

ॐ

The more Jimmy struggled for a solution, the fewer ideas he had.

Two days had passed with no inspiration.

Discouraged and about to give up, he picked up his Bible. Thumbing through the concordance under "Help," Jimmy noticed Psalm 60, verses 11 and 12. He turned to the passage: "Give us help from trouble: for vain is the help of man. Through God we shall do valiantly: for He it is that shall tread down our enemies."

Well, trust the old Bible to call it as it is. He had been

depending on himself, looking in the wrong place for his inspiration.

That night Jimmy went to bed with a certainty in his soul that the solution would come.

❧

Had Imogene not accompanied Miss Goldie the next morning to take her father to the infirmary, she would have gone to the commandant's office. Instead she ran into Gloria in the waiting room.

"I've been looking all over for you," Gloria said, clearly irritated. "Fortunately I saw your sister, and she told me where I could find you."

She was wearing a hot-pink shell with matching shorts and strap sandals. Taking a long draw on her cigarette, she exhaled and flicked a mite of tobacco off her tongue with the long crimson nail of her pinkie. "We need to talk alone. Meet me outside."

Imogene's father was slumped in the side of his chair, his head resting on Miss Goldie's shoulder.

"You go on," Miss Goldie murmured. "I can take care of him." Her worried eyes drifted fondly over his face.

Gloria was leaning against the balustrade at the top of the infirmary steps. "Jimmy wants to see you behind the music building tonight at midnight. He says to be prompt and very careful."

"Do you have any idea—"

Gloria shrugged. "It's up to him to tell you."

"You seem to be his confidante."

"Look—what's between you and Jimmy is your business. What's between me and Jimmy is my business. Let's keep it that way." She flicked an ash into the bushes and sauntered down the steps.

When Gloria first approached her, Imogene's heart had quickened with hope. Now she was not sure, and the woman's studied aloofness gave no clue. If Jimmy was meeting her to tell her he couldn't help, that would be one more day lost. And one day could be crucial.

Had she not been so wary of the commandant, she would have had no choice. She would not have waited until midnight. Now she was torn.

Miss Goldie was alone when Imogene returned to the waiting room.

"It looks as if he has a full-blown case of the measles." She shook her head. "I should have insisted yesterday—"

Imogene patted her hand. "It wouldn't have made an iota of difference. There's really nothing to be done but let it run its course."

"What did Gloria have to say?" Miss Goldie asked.

Imogene paused. "She said Jimmy wanted to see me."

Miss Goldie straightened. "What about?"

"I don't know." That was true enough.

ক

Imogene slipped quietly into her clothes. But she need not have worried; any noise she might have made was masked by Cluny's thundering snores. She tiptoed to the door, peeked out into the empty hall, and skittered silently down the stairs. Heart pounding, she waited in the entry, watching and listening. Then, dashing through the light that flooded the entrance, she darted into the pool of darkness beneath a nearby acacia.

From tree to bush she melded with the shadows as she crossed the spotlit campus. Reaching the music building, she silently slid along the textured wall. Her heart thudded with each twig that snapped beneath her foot.

Something brushed her shoulder.

She whirled around.

"Jim—"

He clamped his hand over her mouth and pulled her to him. "Shh," he whispered urgently.

Locked in his arms, for an instant she forgot her fear. She leaned into his comfort, his strength.

"Oh, Imogene," he murmured, his breath warm against her cheek.

Had she lost her mind?

Violently she pushed him away. "So this is why you brought me out here."

"That's not—"

"Just what did you have in mind?"

Jimmy clamped his hand over her mouth again. "Be quiet, Imogene. Unless you want to bring the whole Japanese army down on us."

What was he going to do, drag her into the bushes and— they already were in the bushes!

"Don't worry—I'm not going to ravage you."

Mind reader.

"I just wanted you to know my plan for getting your sister out of the camp."

Imogene's heart leaped. "Do you mean it?" She was so excited, she hardly even considered saying, *It's about time.* "Oh, Jimmy, I knew you could do it."

"You knew more than I did," he murmured. "And I won't even have to involve the commandant; it's a matter of policy. So simple I can't believe I didn't think of it before."

"Well, tell me."

"Keep your voice down," he warned.

His preamble was driving her crazy.

"Regardless of a woman's citizenship, the Japanese recognize only the husband's," he explained. "In this case, since David Spaneas was a Greek citizen, so is your sister."

"What does that have to do with getting her out?" Imogene asked, hanging on to her patience by a thread.

"If David were alive, she would be released to him. Since he's not, I've arranged that she be released to his family."

"You're a genius!" Imogene could have cried. It was too good to be true. "But what about the fact that he collaborated with the guerrillas?"

"As far as my office goes, I can see that it's kept off the record."

"I can't believe it! How soon can she go?"

"I reached Mr. Spaneas this afternoon. They'll be waiting for her at the gate first thing tomorrow morning."

Impulsively, Imogene threw her arms about his neck. "Oh, Jimmy, I can't tell you how grateful I am. I can't believe it," she repeated softly, resting her cheek against his. It felt so natural, so right to be close to him again.

Jimmy leaned back and looked down at her. In the filtered light of the protective tree, his features were diffused, except for one bright slash of light illuminating his eyes. She had not remembered them quite so dark and velvety.

"Don't discuss this with anyone except your immediate family," he said. "The fewer people who know about it, the less likely there is to be a problem in getting her out. Gloria will meet her just before roll call—"

"Gloria?" A splash of disappointment cooled Imogene's excitement. "What does Gloria have to do with this? I thought you said the fewer people who knew—"

"She knows the protocol and won't be questioned."

Why? Imogene was about to ask when they heard voices. Too late!

The approaching guards they had failed to hear had not failed to hear them. The beam of a flashlight swept the bushes at their feet.

Jimmy jammed her face against his chest, so tight she could hardly breathe.

The light swung up. She could see hers and Jimmy's shadow—one shadow—reflected on the wall behind them.

A guard's harsh, demanding voice rang out. And then he laughed. "Jimmu Yamashida?" He said something in Japanese.

Jimmy responded.

The guard snickered and flicked off the flashlight. As the two walked away, he tossed a remark over his shoulder that amused his companion.

Imogene's knees buckled. Without Jimmy's support, she would have fallen.

"That was close," he whispered.

She clung to him until she could stand, until she had the breath to ask, "What did you say to them?"

"You don't want to know."

"Did you tell them I was a friend of Gloria's?" she ventured.

Jimmy's response was sharp. "Don't ever say anything unkind about Gloria." After some silence, he said quietly, "She needs our prayers, my darling." He stroked Imogene's hair. "More than you know." And then he gently lifted her chin, and she felt his lips on hers.

twenty-one

How often Jimmy had dreamed of this moment. Tentative, he touched his lips to hers, fearful it was a dream yet. But when Imogene's arms tightened around his neck, he knew this was no dream.

He held her close, feeling at last her softness in his embrace. He tasted the sweetness of her lips. He stroked the strands of silken hair cascading through his fingers and breathed in the exotic fragrance of her. He loved her with his whole heart. With every fiber of his being he loved her. For the rest of his life he wanted to be with her, protect her, hold her close as he was doing now.

"Oh, Imogene," he breathed. "Oh, my darling." Reluctantly he pulled back, overwhelmed by the depth of feelings greater than he'd even imagined.

❧

Unable to sleep, Imogene lay on her cot in the slumbering dorm waiting for dawn when she would give Becky the news. She touched her lips, tender from so many kisses. Should she have allowed them? She hadn't refused.

Though she still harbored some small concerns about Jimmy, her trust had largely been restored. How could it be otherwise, after what he'd done for her family? And, although the mere thought of his broad shoulders and kind, handsome face brought palpitations to her heart, she hastened to remind herself that there had always been far more to him than that.

As the pale light of dawn filtered through the high dorm

window, her roommates began to stir. Cluny yawned and stretched and, as usual, reached for a tissue into which she honked indelicately. At their mother's urging, the twins stumbled out of bed and down the hall to be first in the bathroom. Miss Goldie threw back her covers; Becky pulled hers up over her head.

Imogene shook her shoulder. "Becky, get up."

Her sister groaned and rolled over onto her side.

"You've got to hurry. You're getting out of here," Imogene whispered.

"I'm what?" Becky sat up.

"Shh," Imogene whispered and motioned for Miss Goldie to join them. The three huddled together as Imogene told them quietly of the plan.

"But I can't go. What about Daddy?" Becky said.

"What about your baby?" Miss Goldie ran her hand down Becky's tousled hair. "Your father will survive, but if you were to get sick, your baby might not."

"What about both of you?"

"We don't have Greek husbands," Imogene said.

"But I'll miss you," Becky said, her voice uncertain but beginning to relent.

"Not when you get a comfortable bed, clean sheets, and a room of your own," Imogene said. "Besides, you can see me as often as you want. All you have to do is show up at the gate with goodies. So far the Japanese have been very lenient about that."

Becky nodded. "But why didn't you tell me about this before?"

"I didn't know if it could be pulled off. But, thanks to Jimmy, it's happening."

Miss Goldie wagged her head and patted Imogene's hand.

"I hate to say I told you so, but I always saw the goodness in that young man."

Imogene smiled. "So you did, Miss Goldie." She turned to her sister. "Jimmy said the fewer folks who know you're leaving, the better, so whatever you take must fit into a shoe box. The rest you can buy once you're out. Now hustle. Gloria will be here any minute."

"Gloria? What does she have to do with this?"

Imogene shrugged. "When I find out, I'll let you know," she whispered.

A few minutes later, as everyone hurried past on their way to roll call, Gloria waited impatiently for Imogene, Miss Goldie, and Becky to exchange their tearful good-byes.

Gloria took Becky's arm. "You two better get a move on," she said to Imogene and Miss Goldie, "or you'll be late for roll call, and that won't do anybody any good."

A minute later Imogene slipped breathlessly into her place in line, returning a nod to Jimmy's questioning glance. From down the row she caught Angier Duke's curious stare. Hastily, he averted his eyes.

Later that morning, as Imogene was on her way to see her father in the camp hospital, Angier intercepted her.

"Ah, the mailman," Imogene said, not nearly as excited to see him as Daisy's return address on the package he handed her.

"I try to be of help." Angier lowered his eyes modestly. "And it gives me a good feel for what's going on in the camp. I'm thinking of running for the executive committee. I hope I'll have your support."

"Hmm," Imogene murmured, continuing to walk.

As always, Angier fell into step beside her. "I'm hoping you haven't entirely given up the idea of accompanying our chorus."

As always, Imogene accelerated her pace. "I'm afraid my decision will have to wait, now that I'm teaching and with my father sick and all."

Angier hustled along beside her. After a couple of minutes of mutual silence, he said abruptly, "I thought you and that Jap were on the outs."

Imogene's stomach muscles wrenched. "Jap? Whom are you referring to, Angier?" she said sweetly.

"You know very well, Imogene."

They had reached the hospital. "I'm not even going to dignify that with a response," she said over her shoulder as she ran up the steps. It was hard to have Christian thoughts about such an obsequious little snoop. As she walked down the hall, she couldn't help wondering how much Angier knew.

She peeked into her father's room. The light was dim, except for the single beam that shone on an old *New Yorker* magazine from which Miss Goldie was reading aloud.

Imogene's heart lurched. Her once-robust father looked so terribly thin and pale against the white sheets. She couldn't remember ever seeing him sick before, let alone in a hospital bed.

"Hi, Daddy. How are you feeling?"

He shielded his squinting eyes. "Hi, Sweetheart. I'm coming along." His speech was thick and slow. She had to lean down to hear him. "Goldie told me about Rebecca."

"Jimmy was the one who arranged it. Without him, it never could have happened."

Her father managed a small smile. "I hate to say I—"

"I know, 'I told you so.' I've heard that song before." She glanced at Miss Goldie and sat down on the edge of the bed. "Look—I got a package from Daisy." She began to pull off the brown paper wrapping.

"She's a good friend, too," her father said.

"The best." Imogene folded the wrapping for the children's art teacher and rolled up the twine to give to Betty Norton, the twins' mother, who used it to knit afghans. Nothing in the camp was wasted.

Opening the package, Imogene pulled out a box of See's chocolates. "Daisy has her priorities straight—that's for sure. Let's see what else is in here. Mixed nuts. That's good—and some dried fruit." She rummaged around and pulled out a couple of paperback novels. "There has to be a letter here somewhere." She rummaged through the packing material and pulled out an envelope. She tore it open and began reading the note silently to herself.

"Oh, no. Her brother Court's been wounded." Imogene read aloud then: " 'Court was the only member of his platoon to survive, so even though he was wounded, he's lucky to be alive. It's terrible. The doctors can't seem to find what's wrong with him, but he can't walk. They haven't given up hope, nor have I, but sadly Court seems to have. At any rate, the war is over for him.' "

Imogene continued. " 'It is a sad time, Imo, but we have each other. And I believe with all my heart that God is watching over us.' "

Blinking back tears, Imogene folded the letter and stuffed it back in its envelope. Someday this awful war would be over. Where would they all be then? Would she be with Jimmy? Would they go back to America together? She knew she could never recapture the past, even there. Things might look the same, but they would be different. Just as with Court, the scars of war didn't always show.

For several minutes none of them spoke; then Imogene sighed and began to repack the package to carry back to the dorm.

"Gloria stopped in to see how your father was doing," Miss Goldie said.

"Really?"

Miss Goldie nodded. "There was a nurse in here at the time who's a friend of hers."

It's nice to know she has a few lady friends, too. A very unchristian thought that Imogene couldn't suppress.

"Gloria, the poor woman. She lost her fiancé in that first attack of the invasion. It seems they were to be married the following week. Karen—that's the name of the nurse—said Gloria completely changed after that. It's as if she doesn't care whether she lives or dies."

"How tragic." No wonder Jimmy said she needed their prayers. *Judge not, that ye be not judged.* The Bible was filled with lessons she needed to learn, Imogene thought, feeling guilty for her unkind thoughts about Gloria.

Even so, it was no secret Gloria had been more than friendly with some of the officers—even the commandant—and in the back of Imogene's mind, she still couldn't help wondering about Jimmy's relationship with her.

twenty-two

Imogene's father did not improve as expected. His fever continued, and he seemed to grow weaker as they watched. The hospital lacked the drugs to help him.

"We're short on sulfa," the doctor said. "What comes to us through the Red Cross, the Japanese keep for themselves."

"Isn't that against the Geneva Convention?" Imogene asked.

He shrugged. "Tell that to the Japanese."

Maybe Becky would have a resource in Manila. She'd heard how sometimes the sulfa pills were hidden in the skins of bananas and passed to the internees in baskets of fruit.

Becky had settled in with the Spaneases and, even with her expanding girth, made the trek to the main gate of Santo Tomás every other day with fresh produce from their garden. She'd even brought a bouquet of flowers to brighten her father's room. But she hadn't been able to bring the medicine he needed most.

On one of Gloria's visits to see him, she had hinted that she might have a resource. So when she sent a message that she needed to see Imogene, Imogene was quick to respond.

Gloria lived in Franklin Hall on the floor above them. But this was the first time Imogene had visited her room, the only single in the dorm. The advantage of entertaining "friends in high places," Imogene supposed. But ever since Jimmy had said to pray for her, Imogene's attitude had changed toward Gloria. As a result, so had Gloria's toward her.

When she pushed open the door, she was aghast at what

she saw. If she hadn't known it was Gloria's room, she would hardly have recognized the sultry siren beneath the prickly mass of measles covering her bloated face. The woman's eyes were swollen almost shut.

"Oh, Gloria, you poor thing. I'm so sorry. Here you've been nursing everybody else. Now you've got the measles yourself."

"No good deed goes unpunished," Gloria said dryly. Her puffy, inflamed lips barely moved, and her voice came out as a croak. "I'll be okay. . .takes time. . .need you to do me a favor."

"Of course. Anything."

"You can't tell anybody."

"If you say not to."

"It's a medicine drop for the hospital," she whispered.

"Is it dangerous?"

"Well. . .not if you're careful and follow directions exactly."

Excitement skittered up Imogene's spine. "Tell me what to do."

Gloria adjusted the pillow under her head. "You have to be at the back gate at 2:34."

"A.M.?"

"Yeah, A.M. You have only a window of ten minutes between patrols. When you see the gate being unlocked"—she paused to take a couple of slow, deep breaths—"that's your signal. You run over, grab the package"—she breathed again—"and get out of there as fast as you can. Understand?"

Imogene knew she was about to do something important, something that would save lives. Her heart pounded with boldness and the thrill of danger. She repeated Gloria's instructions. "Back gate, 2:34 A.M. But once I've picked up the medicine, what do I do with it then?"

"Karen will be waiting for it at the hospital." Gloria's voice was growing weaker. "Don't give it to anybody else."

"I know Karen—she's one of my father's nurses."

Gloria nodded and closed her eyes. "Be careful."

Imogene touched her shoulder. "Don't worry."

સ

Jimmy waited in the shadows and prayed that everything would go as planned.

For the last several weeks, since there had been a shortage of sulfa in the camp, he had managed to spirit some away from the military hospital's abundant supply, much of which had been designated by the Red Cross for the camp hospital anyway.

That's how he managed to justify his theft. He was stealing from the thieves.

Under the circumstances he figured God would forgive him.

Each time, he prayed the plan would work. So far it had.

The mission couldn't have succeeded without Gloria. She was one of the camp's blessings, although few knew it, especially Gloria herself. He could count on her. She had daring and courage. Sometimes too much. It bordered on recklessness.

"So what?" she'd said. "What more do I have to lose? I've already lost everything that matters to me."

He'd suggested that if she didn't value her own life, at least value his.

Well, if he put it that way, she'd said.

But her cavalier attitude toward danger still made him nervous. For some unaccountable reason, tonight even more than usual.

From his vantage point outside the fence, he had a view of the lighted gate. He heard the guards approach on their way to the barracks and watched them pass. With his pinpoint flashlight, he illuminated his watch. They were on time, almost to the second.

His heart pounded as it always did. So much was at stake.

What if something went wrong? What if the patrol came early or late? What if he or Gloria were to drop the package in their hurried exchange, scattering the contents? What if, what if—

Within the compound he glimpsed movement. Pale skin. A flash of blue.

He hurried to the gate, inserted the key.

That was her signal.

She ran toward him.

It wasn't Gloria!

Imogene!

"Jimmy, what are you—"

He thrust the package into her hands. "Run."

As he relocked the gate, he could hear the voices of the approaching patrol.

He made it to the edge of the woods and sank back into the shadows as they rounded the corner of the compound.

Anxiously he looked back. The area between the fence and the building was empty.

He bent over, resting his hands on his thighs, and sucked in a lungful of air. With a groan of relief, he released it.

Wait until he got his hands on that crazy Gloria! If she chose to risk her own life, that was one thing, but to risk Imogene's? How dare she? And as for Imogene, he was ready to strangle the girl. What did she think she was doing?

All the what-ifs replayed in his mind; all the possibilities of what could have happened added fuel to his outrage. Wait until he got his hands on her.

As he hurried back to his quarters, his anger gradually dissipated, leaving a chord of admiration. Not only was his Imogene beautiful and smart; she was brave.

Nevertheless, he wasn't about to allow her to do it again. Allow her?

Well, he'd do everything he could to discourage her.

❧

Another selfless act of courage from Jimmy. Imogene wanted to sing his praises to the sky; yet she dared not tell a soul.

Standing in line at roll call, she caught his glance and tried to convey her feelings of admiration. What she got in return was a very stern look, which told her how displeased he apparently was with what she had done.

Down the line, as always, Angier's shrewd, knowing stare beamed between them. Wherever Imogene went, he followed her, smothering her with his obsequious concern. Her patience was running thin, if not out.

Several days later, Gloria called Imogene to her room again.

"I hear your father's improved," she said, looking a good deal better herself.

"Thanks to the sulfa. How are you feeling?"

"Better, but I still have a slight fever. Do you think—"

"You want me to do the pickup again? Of course." It would give her another chance to see Jimmy, if only fleeting.

"Jimmy wasn't happy when I sent him the message I was going to ask you again. It seems he doesn't mind risking my life, but yours is a different matter."

Imogene warmed at her words. Of course it wasn't true; he cared for both their safety. It was just that he was in love with Imogene. Her heart skipped. In love with her.

At the appointed hour, Imogene stood in the shadow of the building, her eyes searching the darkness of the woods beyond the fence for some sign of his presence.

She heard the patrol, watched them pass. Breath suspended, she waited.

No flicker in the woods. No Jimmy racing to open the gate.

As the minutes ticked away, she became more and more alarmed.

Had she gotten the time wrong?

No, she was sure not.

The other patrol came and went.

Still no Jimmy.

In her heart Imogene knew something terrible had happened.

twenty-three

Heedless of her safety, Imogene ran across the campus and up the steps of Franklin Hall. She raced up the stairs to the second floor, threw open the door to Gloria's room, and flicked on the light.

"What's the matter?" Gloria sat up in bed, rubbing her eyes.

"Jimmy didn't show up."

"Shut the door—quietly."

"He didn't come," Imogene gasped between breaths. "I waited and waited, and he didn't come. No sign of him. Nothing. Oh, Gloria!" she wailed. "Something awful has happened to him—I know it."

"You don't know it. Pull yourself together." Gloria swung her feet to the floor and put on her robe. "Now sit down and be logical." She gestured toward a straight-back chair at the desk.

"Most likely he simply wasn't able to get the medicine. Maybe someone was in the room where they keep it, or the door was locked. Maybe he was given an assignment by the commandant and couldn't get to the hospital."

She reached over and patted Imogene's hand, which rather surprised Imogene. Gloria wasn't inclined to affectionate gestures.

"He and I agreed, if there was ever any risk, he just wouldn't come. Better to miss one drop-off than ruin a whole operation. Believe me—Jimmy doesn't take unnecessary chances. He drives me crazy the way he's so careful."

"I don't know." Imogene realized she was wringing her hands and lowered them into her lap.

"Trust me—everything's going to be fine."

"I hope you're right, Gloria. I pray you're right."

But when she looked up into Gloria's face, despite the woman's consoling words, Imogene saw concern.

a.

By the time Imogene crawled into bed, it was almost four.

She wondered why she had bothered. No way was she going to fall asleep. Even her eyes refused to close, her gaze darting around the room as restless as her thoughts.

With the first faint splash of dawn across the opposite wall, her spirits lifted a bit. Things never seemed quite so grim in the light of day. Nevertheless, it would be a great relief to see Jimmy at roll call, even if they couldn't speak to each other.

There was the usual early morning rush, people at different paces, lagging and fleet, bumping into each other on the way to the showers or getting dressed. Stumbling out to roll call, they lined up in two straight lines. They stared straight ahead, arms at their sides. And waited.

And waited.

No officers with roll-call sheets.

No Jimmy.

A cord of concern began to tighten around Imogene's heart.

And then the commandant came striding across the lawn, striking a riding crop rhythmically against his thigh. Two soldiers followed. Between them they dragged a third.

Jimmy!

Her knees buckled.

Gasps fluttered down the line.

Instinctively she reached out.

"Don't," the woman beside her muttered and pulled her hand back.

She heard a low, almost guttural moan. Did that come from her?

Oh, my dear Jimmy, what have they done to you?

His chin lolled on his chest, as if he didn't have the strength or will to lift his head. His strong, handsome features were a mass of bruises and cuts, his dark hair matted with blood.

What have they done to you?

His right eye was swollen shut, and an oozing wound from his hairline to the corner of his mouth dripped blood down his cheek and onto his torn shirt. His ripped trousers exposed a slash across his left thigh. His bare bleeding feet were encrusted with dirt.

It took all her will to keep from breaking away, taking him into her arms to comfort him. Comforting herself. She would have, but she knew she would not get two steps before the commandant meted out his retribution on her.

"The commandant wishes me to tell you—"

That voice. Surely not Jimmy's voice, so garbled with pain as to sound less than human.

"—wishes me to tell you. . .yesterday it was called to his attention by someone in the camp that. . .drugs and other medical supplies have been stolen from the military hospital."

Oh, if given the chance, she would run to him and kiss those poor lips until they were smooth and well again.

"The commandant wishes me to tell you—" He sagged and was propped up by the soldiers on either side.

She could hear his mangled breathing as he struggled to speak.

"—wishes to show. . .when emperor defied"—he took another labored breath—"treason." His voice had dwindled to a whisper. "Punishment. . .death. . .day after next."

The stillness was as thick as the humid, tropical air.

Only the incongruous joy of birds warbling in a nearby tree broke the silence.

The commandant barked an order, turned, and strode back across the lawn, slapping his riding crop against his thigh. The two young Japanese soldiers followed in his wake, dragging Jimmy between them.

Almost immediately Miss Goldie was at Imogene's side.

Dazed, Imogene allowed herself to be led toward the dorm. She felt as if she were pushing through water, everything floating and shimmery as she met its resistance.

It could only be a dream. It was too frightening and painful to be real.

She stopped suddenly. "I can't go back to the room, Miss Goldie." Her mouth felt dry as cotton. "All those people— Gloria. We'll tell Gloria. She'll know what to do."

She felt Miss Goldie's comforting arm leading her up the stairs. She heard the murmur of her sweet, consoling voice but was too far into her grief to understand the words.

Miss Goldie knocked on Gloria's door.

"Who is it?"

"Imogene and Goldie Yoder."

"Come in."

Gloria was in her robe, sitting at the desk when they entered. "Oh, no." It was as if the expression on Imogene's face told her what she had feared. "It's Jimmy, isn't it?"

Imogene had held back until this moment. Now she burst into uncontrollable sobs. She fell to her knees, her arms wrapped around herself, and swayed back and forth on the bedroom floor. Tears coursed down her cheeks. She was vaguely aware that Miss Goldie had shut the door and that she and Gloria were now kneeling beside her. She sensed their comforting presence and their wise silence.

They let her rant and wail, until she had used it all up and all that was left was her grief, so deep, so inexplicably deep, that she did not know how she could bear it.

Miss Goldie finally spoke. "You're not alone, Imogene. Remember the Lord's promise, 'I will not leave you comfortless: I will come to you.' He is here now, willing to share your burden, if you'll let Him." She spoke calmly and with such certainty that it would be almost impossible not to trust the truth in her words.

Gloria remained silent, continuing to hold Imogene's hand.

Imogene looked up at her, remembering Gloria's own sadness. How Gloria's young fiancé had been killed in the invasion, just days before they were to be married. Gloria was studying Miss Goldie, and Imogene saw on her face a peace that had not been there before. As if she'd found in Miss Goldie's presence and in her words the comfort that at last she was ready to receive.

Imogene sighed deeply. She wiped her wet cheeks with Gloria's proffered tissue. "We have two days to come up with a plan."

twenty-four

Jimmy lay in the corner of his six-by-eight-foot cell. The pain of his mutilated body was nothing compared to the pain in his heart.

One glimpse of the raw agony on Imogene's face had been enough. To look at her again would have been unbearable. He loved her so much. He'd had such hopes, such plans. He'd dreamed such dreams for them, once the horror of this war was over. The children they would have had, the life they would have shared.

Now there would be only dreams. Ephemeral. Gone like wisps of fog in a murky dawn.

He sighed. For him the horror would soon be over, but what of those he loved. Imogene. His mother and father. How would they take his death?

His father would feel shame, a loss of face.

His mother's heart would be broken, but mended by God's love. His mother would survive. Her foundation ran deep.

Was Imogene's faith deep enough? He raised his eyes heavenward and prayed it was. "Please, God, make it so."

He remembered how his mother had made him copy a verse from Proverbs whenever he'd misbehaved as a boy. She'd always managed to find one to fit the crime. By the time he was ten and had gone away to boarding school, he had accumulated enough for a small book.

"My son, hear the instruction of thy father, and forsake not the law of thy mother." Her personal favorite. He smiled.

If he'd had a son, he'd have taken a page from that book.

If he'd had a son.

"Trust in the Lord with all thine heart; and lean not unto thine own understanding. In all thy ways acknowledge Him, and He shall direct thy paths."

He'd sincerely believed he was on God's path when he took that medicine, knowing the lives it would save.

Was he so misguided? Had he arrogantly gone his own way, telling himself it was God's way? No, he couldn't believe that.

But what had his life amounted to? What did he have to show for it? He was lost to the woman he loved; he had shamed his family, was despised by his country.

Even God seemed to have abandoned him.

He lowered his head, and with a wrenching understanding, he remembered Jesus' words from the cross: "My God, My God, why hast Thou forsaken Me?"

twenty-five

Imogene stood up from the floor and dropped down on the edge of Gloria's bed. "There must be some way to get him out."

Miss Goldie sat down beside her. "Sometimes we have to accept—"

"Miss Goldie, you of all people! Don't give me that 'God's will' business. God gave us a will, too, and He intended for us to use it. Maybe He's testing us as well." Imogene blew her nose. "I'm not going to give up until the last shot is fired—"

Miss Goldie's mouth flew open in horror.

"How about 'The game's not over until the last whistle blows'?" Gloria offered.

Imogene gave her a wan smile. "I think that's better."

Gloria drew the desk chair up beside the bed and sat down. "We have to move fast."

"And we'll need to get outside help," Imogene said.

"What about Rebecca?" Miss Goldie said. "David died protecting the guerrillas. If the family requested it, they might help."

Gloria propped her chin on her fist. "For this to work we also have to get inside help." Her lips curved up in a small, secretive smile. "I think I can handle that."

Both Imogene and Miss Goldie gave her an oblique look.

"Not the way you're thinking. I have some money stashed away—" Gloria stood and slid the chair back under the desk. "You handle the break-in; I'll handle the bribe."

"We'll think of it as tithing," Miss Goldie said primly.

Imogene rose. "It's settled then. I'm meeting Becky at the

gate in an hour. I'll fill her in on our plan."

Although despair still hung heavy in her heart, she felt some relief in being able to take action.

At the door she paused. "Remember yesterday you said Jimmy wasn't happy when he found out I was the one going to meet him? How did he find out it was to be me instead of you?"

"I sent him a note."

"Who delivered it?"

❧

Imogene was waiting for him when he rounded the corner of the dorm.

"Oh, my dear Imogene. Isn't it just dreadful what happened to Jimmy?" Angier wrung his hands. "It makes me heartsick."

"You Judas!" She spat. She was almost blind with fury.

Angier's mouth dropped open into a surprised O. "Why, why, what do you mean?"

"You know what I mean."

"You don't think I had anything—"

"Don't you lie to me." Her heart was pumping so fast, she could hardly breathe. "I already know who 'brought it to the commandant's attention'—*Mr. Postman!*"

A nerve in Angier's cheek jumped; his mouth twitched. "All right, so I did bring it to the commandant's attention." His gaze darted past her. "So what? Jimmy's a Jap like any other Jap. What's the loss?"

She clenched her fists. She wanted to smash his prissy little face into a bloody pulp.

She wanted to kill him.

Oh, God. Oh, dear God.

She closed her eyes and pulled her clasped hands up to her face, struggling to control the savage hate raging inside her.

Dear God, help me.

Vengeance is mine. . .saith the Lord.

The words rang in her ears and in her mind and finally in her heart. A great sense of relief came over her.

"But why? Why did you do it? It wasn't because he was Japanese. He was trying to help us."

Angier's demeanor changed. He didn't answer at once. He shuffled his feet. "I—because I—" His gaze darted to her face and then to the ground. "Because I love you. I've always loved you. Oh, Imogene—" He stretched out his hand, beseeching.

God had answered her prayer. Looking at the pathetic mass of whimpering tics, her anger dissipated. She felt only pity.

"I just wanted him to leave you alone. I didn't think—"

"No, you didn't think, Angier," she said quietly.

After a moment he whispered, "Are you going to tell anybody?"

Imogene paused, then shook her head. "No, I'm not going to tell. I wouldn't want what might happen to you to be on my conscience."

Angier's head lowered, his gaze focused on the ground near her shoe.

"I don't have to punish you, Angier. I don't have to judge you. God will do that." Her voice was calm. "I don't envy you. If there is a hell on earth, for as long as you live, you will be in it, remembering what you did to Jimmy."

She left him standing in a sun that, for him, would be ever darkened.

❧

It was done. The plan was in place.

Imogene had confronted her outrage with Angier, and now all that was left was to talk to her father.

She found him in his bathrobe sunning in the patio of the infirmary. Though far from his old robust self, since receiving the medicine, he was at least on the mend.

Miss Goldie sat next to him crocheting a baby sweater she hoped would be finished before Becky delivered—which could be any day.

"You're going to have to work fast, Miss Goldie," Imogene said.

When her father saw her, he held out his arms.

As she had when she was a child, and ever since, she ran into them. Those strong, comforting arms that were always there for her, and always would be, no matter what happened.

"Goldie told me about Jimmy," he said.

Imogene nodded, fighting back tears. Her father and Miss Goldie didn't know it yet, but it might be a long time before they saw each other again—if ever.

"Did she tell you the plan?"

"It sounds risky. What do you think are the chances?"

Imogene shrugged. "What is it you always say—it's in God's hands now. Daddy—"

"Yes, Honey."

"I'm going with him."

The crochet hook dropped from Miss Goldie's fingers and clattered onto the cement.

Her father looked at Imogene without moving.

"I've made up my mind."

He expelled a deep breath. "There's nothing I can say?"

She shook her head. "Gloria has arranged everything." Imogene gave a sardonic smile. "She has friends in high places, you know. She's good, Daddy. In her heart she's so good. She needs friends like you and Miss Goldie."

Miss Goldie leaned forward. "We are her friends, Imogene—you know that."

"I do."

"You're sure there's nothing that will convince you not to go?" her father asked.

"Nothing, Daddy."

Miss Goldie's small hand covered his. "We understand." Her gaze met his.

Imogene ached at the look of love exchanged between them.

"There is one more thing we can do, though." Miss Goldie reached for Imogene's hand.

Fingers intertwined, Imogene, her father, and Miss Goldie bowed their heads in one last prayer.

❧

The cell door banged shut behind her. The lock engaged. The guard's booted feet echoed down the hall into silence.

Imogene's stomach roiled at the repugnant odors that assaulted her. Her eyes struggled to adjust to the muted light, its source a narrow strip at the top of the door.

On the floor in the corner of the cell, a form moved.

"Jimmy, it's me," she whispered.

"Imogene?" His voice was raspy and uncertain.

"Oh, Jimmy, oh, my darling." Oblivious to the stench and filth, she fell to her knees beside him. Gently she gathered him close and drew his head against her heart, cradling him, rocking him back and forth as she would a child. "I'm with you now, Darling. I'm never going to leave you."

"How—?" He tried to lift his head, but it fell back against her chest.

"Shh. It doesn't matter. I'm here now. And soon, my darling, you'll be free."

She had no idea how long she held him, soothing him, while her own heart beat with anxiety and excitement.

It seemed forever.

Finally, outside the cell, she heard the clink and scrape of a key being inserted into the lock and then the slow, grinding music of rusted hinges as the door slid open.

In the rectangle of light stood three figures clad in U.S. Army fatigues.

They moved forward, making no sound. Two picked up Jimmy, signaling Imogene to follow. The third brought up the rear as they hurried silently down the hall.

Heart pounding, she kept pace, urged on by the man behind her. Once out of the barracks, they raced across the open space and along the fence, then, hunkering down, skirted through a section that had been previously cut.

Everything was going according to plan.

Gloria had done her part. No guard in sight.

Imogene could see the faint silhouette of a truck hidden in a copse of trees a few paces beyond the campground. As they approached, she heard the low rumble of its idling motor.

They laid Jimmy on a blanket in the truck bed and lifted her up after him. As she sank down beside him, she felt a tremendous sense of relief, but also gratitude. Gratitude to all those who had risked their lives to help them, people who knew them and those who didn't, like these brave guerrillas sitting beside her. But most especially she thanked the Almighty, for giving her the resources and showing her the path.

Suddenly the truck was flooded with light.

Sirens screamed a deafening, intermittent warning.

She heard the spit of shots from every direction and felt the whiz of a bullet, close as an eyelash.

The truck lurched forward, accelerated, lunging headlong into the darkness.

She threw herself across Jimmy's body, and as she did, a sharp, excruciating pain ripped through her.

I'm going to die, she thought, as she slipped into oblivion.

twenty-six

Jimmy's view from the lookout post on the north ridge offered a spectacular panorama of a sky that seemed to lift to heaven and a jungle that spread like a green carpet beneath it. He adjusted the lenses on his binoculars and lowered his sights, sweeping the lake a thousand feet below, the coconut groves, and the rice paddies along its banks for enemy patrols. From this vantage point, the water looked calm and the jungle deceptively still.

How could he possibly have imagined, as a college student in California, that he would one day be the lone Japanese soldier fighting in a band of Filipino and American guerrillas—against his own people?

Dear God. He tried not to think about that. He just tried to live each day as it came and do his duty as he understood it.

They'd gotten word that Japan was being bombed. He feared for his parents. If they had managed to get to their mountain house, there was a chance they were safe.

Many islands had fallen back into American hands, but when were they going to repatriate the Philippines? For three years this territory had been under Japan's tyrannical domination. Why had the Americans waited so long? With each day more died.

So many killed in this war. So much death.

"Lord, so much death."

"Hey, you losing it, Buddy?" Steve Putnam, a redheaded soldier from Idaho, his replacement, clambered up onto the

162

ridge. "Talking to yourself?"

Jimmy handed over the binoculars. "No, old man, talking to God."

***

February 3, 1945

The early morning sun was bright, and the air redolent with the loamy smell of rich, damp earth. A profusion of vines clambered over the rough wood shack and swung loosely in the cool breeze. Orchids peeked from hidden places. Air plants clung to the surrounding trees, the weight of their branches supported by buttresses that extended from their thick trunks.

In the shack, Jimmy rolled over and nuzzled the back of Imogene's neck as she lay on her tummy beside him. "So, Mrs. Yamashida, any regrets after two years of marriage?"

"Mmm, not if you keep that up," she murmured sleepily.

He kissed the scar on her shoulder. "That little piece of business almost took you from me."

"But it didn't." Languidly, she turned toward him, luxuriating in the kisses he rained over her cheeks and down her throat, ending in that tender spot behind her ear.

It was their second year of marriage, but they were still in their honeymoon cottage, a three-sided shack in a guerrilla compound deep in the jungle above Manila.

"Becky was prepared to see me at my worst that night," Jimmy said. "She didn't expect to find you even worse. She took a big risk keeping us at her house that long."

"So did Dr. Crawford." Imogene kissed his nose.

"Ah, yes, the multitalented Dr. Crawford, medical missionary and minister, all in one."

"Saved my life and my reputation." Imogene giggled.

Jimmy propped himself up on one elbow and looked down

at her, a serious expression in his eyes. "I want us to have a baby, Immie."

"It won't be long now, Darling. From all the news we're getting, war will soon be over."

Oh, how she loved him. He was everything she'd hoped for in a man and in a husband. Aside from his passionate nature, he demonstrated the depth of his love and respect in small acts of courtesy and kindness. "I can hardly wait to see what kind of father you'll make."

"Me either." He flopped over onto his back. "I feel bad when I think of David Spaneas, never being able to know his son."

Imogene ran her fingers down his cheek. "I like to think he does," she said softly. "Davy's two and a half years old—can you believe it?"

They lay on their backs, their fingers touching, thinking their own thoughts.

"I'm glad your dad finally made an honest woman of Miss Goldie," Jimmy mused, smiling.

"Me, too. I was really beginning to worry about her reputation." Imogene chuckled. "Speaking of reputations, I wonder what happened to Gloria?"

"We'll have to ask Becky the next time we can manage to get a message to her."

"Our link to the outside world, what there is left of it."

Imogene sat up. "Do you hear that?"

"Yes. Sounds kind of like a hive of bees." He looked at her. "You don't suppose—"

She jumped out of bed. "It's getting louder."

Jimmy was beside her. "They're airplanes, Imogene."

They ran down the steps into the front clearing and looked in the direction from which the noise came. Louder and louder it grew until their small hut shook in the deafening roar, and in that patch of sky overhead, American bombers in formation blotted out the rising sun.

General MacArthur was coming back, just as he said he would.

Tears of joy streamed unchecked down both their cheeks. Jimmy pulled Imogene close.

The war would soon be over.

epilogue

Ten months later

The house was bright and polished as the day when they had left it, and most of the family treasures Imogene's father had distributed among the servants, expecting never to see his beloved plantation again, had been returned and were in their appointed places.

Emotions close to the surface since his illness, he wept.

It was a week after they had arrived, and the family was assembled in a circle of lawn chairs on that patch of lawn where four and a half years earlier Imogene had waved good-bye to Bertha and Lupe.

Soon she would be doing so again.

Tomorrow she and Jimmy were boarding a ship for Japan.

"I anticipate a beautiful reunion with your family," Miss Goldie said. She was still Miss Goldie to everybody—except her husband—even though she had been married for almost two years. "I know they'll be so relieved to see you're still fit and handsome. In spite of everything you went through."

"We all went through," Jimmy said, absently stroking Imogene's arm.

Becky, on the other side of Imogene, handed her son, Davy, a cookie. "How do you think that father of yours is going to feel about your being a Christian missionary, Jimmy?"

Jimmy shrugged, as he almost always did when his dad was mentioned. "He'll get used to it. It's my Father in heaven I'm concerned about pleasing." He looked fondly at Imogene. "My mother's going to love you."

"Well, it's your father I'm worried about," Imogene said. "But I think I might be able to win him over."

"He's never approved that much of me—what gives you the edge?"

"Because I'm going to give him a grandchild."

"You're what?" Jimmy's mouth fell open. "Imogene." He leaped from his chair and grabbed her up into his arms. "Why didn't you tell me?"

"What do you think I'm doing now? I just found out myself."

"I'm going to be a dad." His voice was filled with awe.

"And I'm going to be a granddad." Imogene's father, who'd seemed to be dozing in the chair next to Miss Goldie, sat up.

"Oh, Imo, that's wonderful!" Becky sprang out of her chair and hugged them both.

Miss Goldie was almost as quick.

Davy ran over to his grandfather and threw his arms wide. "You a-ready a grampa."

The older man swept the little boy up in a bear hug. "So I am, Davy boy."

"And you'll always be our favorite first grandchild, Mr. Davy," Miss Goldie said.

"I know that." Davy looked down and pointed at the plate of cookies sitting on the small table between his grandfather and grandmother. "Can I have a cookie?" Apparently he'd had enough of this baby business.

"I can't believe it!" Jimmy put Imogene down. "You're sure?"

"Well, if she's not, I am." A dark-haired woman strolled down the front steps.

Imogene ran over and grabbed Gloria's hand, drawing her

into the group. "Isn't it clever of us to take along our own private nurse?"

"That's what you think," Miss Goldie said. "When you all get to the mission, you'll have plenty of folks to share her with."

Imogene smiled at the attractive woman in the modest blue chemise. It looked as if Gloria was well on the road to redemption.

"I hear you're leaving, too, Becky," Gloria said.

Becky nodded. "The Spaneases were wonderful. They wanted me to stay. But I just couldn't. It was too painful, all the memories. I thought it was time for Davy and me to make a new beginning. So when Imo's college friend Daisy offered—"

"*Begged* is more like it," Imogene said.

Becky cast her an oblique look and shrugged. "Anyway, she needs a housekeeper and companion for her brother, Court, who's in a wheelchair. I thought it would be perfect for Davy and me. Room, board, and a great salary. And I don't have to stay more than a year if I don't want to. So yesterday I sent her a letter and said I'd take it. They're even paying for our passage. First class."

"They can afford it," Imogene assured her.

Miss Goldie sat back down in her chair and pulled a hankie from the sleeve of her blouse. She sniffed and wiped her eyes. "God has been so good to us. Here we are all together. We have one beautiful baby—"

"I'm not a baby, Gramma. I'm a boy."

Miss Goldie smiled at the dark-haired, cherub-faced tot in his grandfather's lap. "One handsome boy," she corrected, "and expecting another grandchild. And you're all"—she blew her nose daintily into the linen hankie—"you're all going to leave us. Don't misunderstand. I couldn't be happier for you.

It's just that I'm going to miss you so very much. You're the only family I have."

It was a bittersweet moment.

"You have me, Goldie," her husband said, his eyes twinkling. "And an entire plantation of workers to look after. What more could a woman ask for?"

Miss Goldie paused, then straightened. "You're right, Will. Now that I'm sending two missionaries to replace me." She smiled at her husband.

From the vantage of Jimmy's arms, Imogene's gaze fell on each of them in turn, her father and Miss Goldie, Becky, Davy, Gloria. She knew that no matter what distance lay between them, they would always be close, bound by the love of God and of each other.

Acknowledgments

I thank my family and friends for encouragement and support, especially my husband, Charles, who does much more than go over my work with his red pencil. For lending me Aunt Alice Bryant's book *The Sun Was Darkened,* a chronicle of her years interned with my uncle Will in Santo Tomás, I thank my cousin Imogene Williams, their daughter and my heroine at age seven, who lived with us during those years and introduced me to "yummy gookums." And, finally, I acknowledge Sofia Adamson's book *Gods, Angels, Pearls and Roses,* which allowed me insight into the city of Manila during those dark days.

A Letter To Our Readers

Dear Reader:

In order that we might better contribute to your reading enjoyment, we would appreciate your taking a few minutes to respond to the following questions. We welcome your comments and read each form and letter we receive. When completed, please return to the following:

Rebecca Germany, Fiction Editor
Heartsong Presents
PO Box 719
Uhrichsville, Ohio 44683

1. Did you enjoy reading *Dark Side of the Sun* by Rachel Druten?
   ❑ Very much! I would like to see more books by this author!
   ❑ Moderately. I would have enjoyed it more if

   _____

   _____

   _____

2. Are you a member of **Heartsong Presents?** ❑ Yes ❑ No
   If no, where did you purchase this book? _____

   _____

3. How would you rate, on a scale from 1 (poor) to 5 (superior), the cover design? _____

4. On a scale from 1 (poor) to 10 (superior), please rate the following elements.

   ____ Heroine   ____ Plot
   ____ Hero   ____ Inspirational theme
   ____ Setting   ____ Secondary characters

6. How has this book inspired your life?_____

_____

_____

7. What settings would you like to see covered in future
   Heartsong Presents books? _____

_____

_____

8. What are some inspirational themes you would like to see
   treated in future books? _____

_____

_____

9. Would you be interested in reading other **Heartsong
   Presents** titles? ❑ Yes ❑ No

10. Please check your age range:
   ❑ Under 18   ❑ 18-24
   ❑ 25-34   ❑ 35-45
   ❑ 46-55   ❑ Over 55

Name _____

Occupation _____

Address _____

City_____ State_____ Zip_____

E-mail _____

HEARTSONG ♥ PRESENTS
Love Stories
Are Rated G!

That's for godly, gratifying, and of course, great! If you love a thrilling love story but don't appreciate the sordidness of some popular paperback romances, **Heartsong Presents** is for you. In fact, **Heartsong Presents** is the only inspirational romance book club featuring love stories where Christian faith is the primary ingredient in a marriage relationship.

Sign up today to receive your first set of four, never-before-published Christian romances. Send no money now; you will receive a bill with the first shipment. You may cancel at any time without obligation, and if you aren't completely satisfied with any selection, you may return the books for an immediate refund!

Imagine. . .four new romances every four weeks—two historical, two contemporary—with men and women like you who long to meet the one God has chosen as the love of their lives. . .all for the low price of $10.99 postpaid.

To join, simply complete the coupon below and mail to the address provided. **Heartsong Presents** romances are rated G for another reason: They'll arrive Godspeed!

YES! Sign me up for Heart♥ng!